THE NOTHING THAT IS

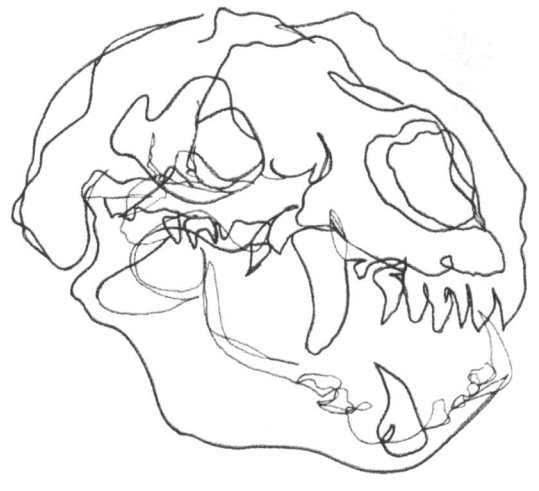

KYLE WINKLER

The Nothing That Is

Copyright © 2021 by Kyle Winkler

All rights reserved. No part of this book may be reproduced in any form by any electronic or mechanical means including photocopying, recording, or information storage and retrieval without permission in writing from the author.

ISBN-13: 979-872204-495-2

Cover design by Ryan Dunn (Instagram: @dunnhog)

Interior layout by Scott Cole (www.13visions.com)

Edited by Erin Al-Mehairi (hookofabook@hotmail.com)

Interior drawings by Claudia Lundahl

First Edition

kylewinkler.net

Twitter: @bleakhousing

For all my brothers, sisters, comrades, and folx who have worked, are working, or will work in the Food Service Industrial Complex.

And to anyone who's ever had an asshole boss.

An armchair presupposes the human body, its joints and limbs; a pair of scissors, the act of cutting. What can be said of a lamp or a car? The savage cannot comprehend the missionary's Bible; the passenger does not see the same rigging as the sailors. If we really saw the world, maybe we would understand it.

Jorge Luis Borges, "There Are More Things"

...he must have a long spoon that must eat with the devil.

Shakespeare, *The Comedy of Errors*

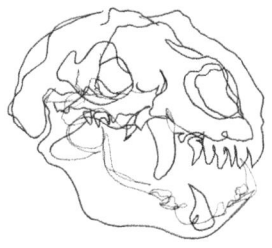

ONE

The graveyard exploded.

Part of it, anyway.

That's how it started. I was driving to work, and on the other side of town, the graveyard exploded. I felt it through my chest. My busted-ass dashboard rattled. The quarters in the console jingled. The hot weak McDonald's coffee splashed over the cup holder.

I thought maybe we were getting that massive earthquake, you know? The Earth Splitter. That New Madrid Fault Line ran like a seam down between Illinois and Indiana into Kentucky. I'd heard we could expect a shake bigger than anything California ever suffered.

A bit later, the radio station (WRBT the Frog) dropped the Madonna song and the Morning DJ read a sterile announcement from the police about a suspected natural gas leak ignited by an eternal flame at a memorial in the Golden Forest Cemetery.

Golden forest.

Sounds sick, but I laughed at the cruel thought of a graveyard bursting and spewing out corpses. The point of eternal rest was to sleep a long time.

To be fair, it was early, crazy-early on a Monday, and I'd gotten little sleep over the weekend. Like, zero.

I kept having these dreams that I was sitting by a cold fire—flames that held no heat.

I worked for Starboard Catering Services, Inc. It was an independent but successful regional business based out of Indianapolis, IN. Such a thing as independent catering may sound a bit outdated, but around 1986 (when what I'm about to tell you went down) we did brisk business. Lots of unregulated corporate income went to spending on lavish five course meals for CEOs and ass-kissing middle managers.

We fed computer developers, toy manufacturers, electronics magnates. Yes, we had technology even in the soon-to-be Rust Belt. In our dinky southwestern Indiana river town, we had two integrated circuit board factories. We catered for them twice a month.

You could say I was busy.

I instinctively pressed the play button on the answering machine when I got into the manager's office. I hated touching that machine. It shined with grease like a lumpy animal organ. Cords sticking out. It was filthy. Abused, too, with various condiment stains from unwashed fingers. And it had been broken for at least a week. I was surprised that any messages even recorded. I listened to the new one twice. It was hard to decipher.

BEEP! [something something] *business* [something] *extreme food* [something] *thank you* (phone number) *BEEP!*

I usually arrived first in the mornings. Folks called it the Assistant Manager's Curse. Unlock at 4:30 a.m., leave around 5 p.m. Not glamorous. I organized the day's menus into binders. Shuffled next month's employee schedules. Made copies. Faxed a few inventory requests to suppliers. Played the message again. The guy's voice on the machine was garbled but calm. Almost soothing. I stared out the office windows into the big, industrial kitchen. The gargantuan mixing urns. The stacks of warming ovens and flattop grills as big as mattresses. Rows of wide worktables. Magnetized bars with magically clinging knives. All of it stainless and shiny. All of it like sleeping metal beasts. My employees grinded their asses off to keep that kitchen spotless. And here the management team couldn't keep their goddamn desks free of barbecue sauce. The catering world collected all kinds, I supposed.

An image of that cold fire from my dream invaded my head. To concentrate, I stared at an autographed headshot of the actress Donna Douglas. I actually hated *The Beverly Hillbillies* but Elly May Clampett was cute. Once, for some reason, Ms. Douglas was in our retrograde town and graced a catering job we did. She signed pictures like they were gold bricks. I took one—what the hell.

"Thanks for the vicutals!" Donna wrote in blue marker underneath her name.

Victuals. What a weird word. I had been in catering for five years at that point and never heard that word. I looked it up once, and it was a fancy word for "food."

Next to the picture was a small fishbowl where my betta fish, Curly, swam around. I dabbed in some flakes. He'd been sluggish lately.

I played the message one more time. I took a stab at the phone number to try and call back. If I didn't figure the message out, and my boss Andy Rodnicki heard it, he'd skewer my head to the punch clock. Rodnicki was a stooge. But he ran the show. I had to bend the knee if I wanted to keep my job. No one liked Rodnicki, but he won people over through gregarious attrition. He had slicked back hair, black beard, lots of hand gestures. He lead with his paunch. Everyone could hear the *klik-klak* of his dress shoes on the kitchen tiles.

Rodnicki was a shithead, but upbeat about it.

It was hard to fight against.

I was, I think, the only one to know that he was skimming the books. His wife was the comptroller, and they'd had money issues in the past. But when she took over, their financial futures looked, let's say, more sanguine. Our finances never leapt like they should've. Here I was scrounging to get new clients with bigger gigs and create and develop more interesting menus and dishes, but Rodnicki and his wife embezzled their way into sleazy security. No way. What's more, we were starting to get "professional notes" from the higher-ups in Indy asking why our holiday numbers weren't doing well. What was the answer? Rodnicki had none. He'd pawn these notes off to me and make an excuse about being in a meeting.

I was a smear of an Assistant Manager. Would I go above my boss to the District Manager? Again, no way. More like Corporate would slice off my ears and serve them back to me with a lemon wedge and a parsley sprig.

In the end, I figured I'd wait it out. Rodnicki and Lorraine would stumble at some point when the District Manager performed an audit or asked for the bookkeeping. Something would surface. But, both life preservers and dead bodies float.

Maybe I should've conjured a different metaphor there.

Anyway, the kitchen staff loved me, respected me. I jived with everyone. But with Rodnicki at the top, I couldn't go anywhere. I was stuck. And I'd bought into the idea from my old man that once you started a project, or a job, you stuck with it until the end. Which was always bullshit, right? He never stayed in one job longer than a few years. The sharpened points of advice from adults quickly lost any standing with me by the time middle school rolled around. Everyone chained to capitalism wanted to view their job as being a part of building some massive cathedral over multiple generations. But in reality it was more like building a temporary outhouse near a battlefield.

One of Starboard's long-time chefs, Big Tiny Keller, said I should start my own catering business. He'd abandon Starboard and join me. Stick it up the company's ass, etc. He was serious, too. He suggested this once a week as we'd stand on the dock and he smoked. I mused on it, a lot. I dreamed about it, even planned for it. But with what money?

I dialed the number I heard in the message. The line rang, rang. Nothing. A minute of ringing. Then a beep. I left my info, this is Cade McCall, Asst. Blah, for Blah Blah Catering, I was returning your blah about your message. Please call back at—and here, I cannot explain what happened—I rattled off a phone number.

But it was not the office number.

It was my home number.

Why? Why did I do that? I have no idea what compelled me to do that. It just *happened*. I hung up too late to correct it. I called back and left another message with the right number. Same patter, same beige tone.

About three hours later, Rodnicki strolled in, late as usual. Now my office phone rang. His line was blinking. He was too lazy to walk the fifteen feet to my office. He summoned us all like he was a king. (He voted for Reagan twice. *Twice.*) I answered the phone. It was his wife, Lorraine.

"Rise and shine, rooster."

Jesus. I'd been here while they were asleep.

"On my way," I said, hung up, cursed, stood, cursed again.

His office was a cramped but private room next to the mop closet.

"What's up, McCall? Smile for god's sake. It's Monday. Let's give these goofballs something to look up to. You feel that shit earlier? The cemetery? What a mess. Lorraine says her friend saw the bodies and caskets laying all over the place when she drove by. You believe that? Insurance will be all over 'em."

I never engaged in Rodnicki's gossip, of which there was a truckload. I handed him the day's menus, the upcoming gig-sheets, and a handful of new applications. My preferred hires had stars by their names. We forever needed fresh bodies. Young, energetic kids happy to peddle platefuls of food for minimum wage and tips. Preferably local college kids or mature high schoolers. They always got free meals out of it. Nothing like building outhouses next to battlefields, right?

He'd maybe skim the day's menus. The rest would take an agonizing week to review.

Instead of looking at anything, Rodnicki gassed on about how pathetic our city was for letting a cemetery blow up. But it wasn't large-hearted concern for the families of the deceased. No. He was more concerned about dead bodies getting into the sewers or something. Lorraine complained that the water would be tainted with embalming fluid.

These people were my superiors. Luckily, it was easy to ignore them. Nod and Yup.

I fixated on giving out my home number to that cracked-out caller. What the hell was going on? I blamed it on the graveyard explosion. It rattled more than my change and coffee. My head was blasted. And then I noticed the Mondale/Ferraro button Rodnicki stole from my desk. Pinned to his corkboard. Such a stooge—

"Fucking pay attention, McCall. Messages?"

Goddamn it.

Rodnicki was standing now. Faux emperor. Behind him, his emperorette was perched on a typewriter table without a typewriter. She off-loaded all the serious typing to our shift managers, natch.

"Machine's still busted."

"Well, Jesus H. Christmas, get a new one."

"You said Lorraine was going to order it."

Lorraine blushed. I caught him for a second. And her. But he pivoted.

"Don't blame her. You're the assistant manager, which means you manage the office affairs, too."

Not true. The comptroller did that, but whatever. I said I'd get a new answering machine and left. Which meant I'd have to take time out of my lunch break to go to the office supply store. More time away from Rodnicki was time well spent.

The red, white, and blue image of that Mondale/Ferraro button burned into my brain. I was going to get that damn piece of plastic back.

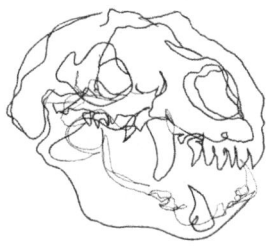

TWO

The rest of the Monday melted away. Every day in catering wipes you out. We made two hundred and fifty filet mignons and three hundred lobster thermidors.

When I dragged myself home and saw my own answering machine was blinking, I figured it was Rodnicki leaving me some extra ass-chewing. Guy probably argued with his shampoo.

I let the machine blink.

I popped a Stroh's and watched a documentary on PBS about the Cretaceous era. Some beers later, I remembered the message and felt girded enough to listen.

That strange, calm, garbled request had followed me home.

My machine wasn't caked in grease, but the button felt slippery slick. I can't believe the weirdo called my home and hadn't listened to my follow-up message. The tape chirped and the same wobbly, croaking voice plead in the most plangent tones for me to take their catering order. The gig was for nine people, including himself (no name given), and he would pay, no lie, get this: $1,000 a head. I smashed my thumb onto the rewind button. *I would be delighted to remunerate your services for one thousand dollars a person.* That part I heard quite clearly. Tipsy, or let's be honest, entry-level drunk, I didn't care, I called the number from memory.

Someone picked up on the first ring. The Calm Guy. He explained over again what he wanted. I said that it was technically outside working hours, but I didn't want to lose his business. Could he call the office tomorrow? He wondered if I could entertain his request first. He had *unusual* terms. I snagged a pad and pencil and told him to shoot. The list started promising. New potatoes with rosemary. Pork medallions. Roasted asparagus. Corn chowder. Garden salads. This was insane. They were willing to pay ten times our asking price for the Catering Basics. The Catering Top Five. "Money for nothing..." as the hit song on the radio crooned.

"Now, I wonder if you can access snake carcasses."

"Pardon? Can you repeat that?"

"Snake carcasses. We prefer viper meat. But honestly any snake will do. If one has no choice." The voice almost dropped a whole register. Like two men were speaking at the same time.

"You're kidding, right? This is a joke."

Silence.

One thousand dollars a head.

"You know," I said, "I know a guy who does snake stuff. A snake hunter type fella. Yeah. I'll get hooked up with him. No problem. We'll make it work." I'd never seen a viper in my life, let alone been anywhere near a snake since a child at the zoo. But I thought Big Tiny Keller did taxidermy in his spare time. Maybe he could help.

"Good," the caller said.

There were some other small items, but he had them and would, perhaps, drop them off for us to incorporate into the dishes. Spices and whatnot. I asked what this was for. Who should I say was the client. I needed a name for the gig sheet. He said they were an extreme food club. Met once a month. Always trying at least one eccentric food. This week: snake. I didn't mention this, but I'd heard of people eating snake before. Tastes like chicken, right?

Then I said again I needed a contact name to go with the number. And a place to bill them. There was a duration of static where I felt like the voice on the other end of the line could be standing right around the corner from me. As if they were up against my pantry or hallway. The breathing on the line wasn't *in* my ear the way a call usually is. The breathing was *behind* my ear somehow. That voice that sounded like two voices layered on top of one another. One voice wearing another voice like a sleeve.

I turned. I'd not had any lights on except the TV. It was me and the tube and the recliner.

"Make up a name," the man said. I didn't follow. "What's on your television set?"

"A documentary about dinosaurs."

"I'm Mr. Dinosaur."

Where were we doing this? Mr. Dinosaur gave an address. A rural route number, past the college, past the steel mill. It was the Toothaker Estate, an old fraternity house that was then converted into an Elks lodge. Now it was in private hands. I think I'd been invited to a gala there once years ago. Didn't attend. Before I asked about payment, Mr. Dinosaur said I could be paid tomorrow, if need be. In our preferred method.

Again—unthinking—I blurted, "Make a check out to cash. Leave it in an envelope addressed to me at the catering office."

And again, that double-layered breath *behind* the ear.

"Very good," and Mr. Dinosaur hung up.

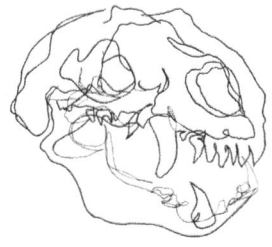

THREE

The graveyard explosion dominated all local conversation for a solid week. It got a regular spot on the nightly eleven o'clock news. The first report aired after I talked to Mr. Dinosaur. Clean up crews, special kinds with hazardous waste suits, were called in from around the state. Families congregated, preparing lawsuits, re-burials, and so on. I hated to think of it, but I wondered who would need catering services. I stowed the thought away.

The next morning, I got in at 4:30 a.m., and there was an envelope. I couldn't believe that someone would be willing to pay that much for a gig. Yet there it was, leaning against the dock's double doors—a stained, old envelope. Almost like it was oily from a long time at the bottom of a steamer trunk. Mr. Dinosaur had skipped the check and instead there was eleven thousand dollars in large bills and a small hand-written note. The note said: *The extra two thousand is for helping us in such short notice. Please bring industrial strength cleaner.* I looked around, as if a security guard or a police officer would be ready to snatch it away. Or Lorraine Rodnicki with her narrowed eyes, scheming a way to fleece the money off me.

I mean, technically what I was doing—what I was aiming to do—was illegal. But I had devised a plan. I would tell this Mr. Dinosaur person that I'd decided to work independently. The question was: would this person care? Would his Extreme Food Club care? Eleven thousand would go a long way as collateral for my own catering business.

I pocketed the envelope and an electric thrill shot from my feet to that small point on the top of my scalp. That tingle wouldn't leave for hours. Didn't even need coffee. I danced with that natural juice, that excitement. Later in the morning, Big Tiny Keller asked twice what was up with me. Snapping his tongs at me like a creature feature. "Did you win the lottery or get lucky?" he said. He stroked his handlebar mustache. He was a former biker who had a talent in the kitchen. He was driven, took absolutely zero shit, and knew how to whip up both meatloaf and eggs Florentine. I'd need him for the gig.

I asked him if we could grab a smoke over lunch. He winked. "Troublemaker. I like it. Let's get rowdy."

It wasn't until after I'd gotten stuck into some paperwork at my desk that I noticed Curly. He was sunk near the bottom, unmoving. My Eleven Thousand Dollar Thrill plummeted. I panicked. I did the thing you're not supposed to do to fish tanks. I flicked it. Instead of pissing Curly off, my flick untethered him from some unseen force and his tiny purple iridescent body bloated upward. The little guy was dead. Now, I had small cause for serious grief here. I know that. But I also knew that betta fish usually lived for years. Curly was maybe eight months old.

Fuckery was afoot.

I opened the top of his tiny tank to scoop him out and stopped. There was white scum coating the top of the water. Maybe it was pure paranoia, but my first thought was that Lorraine had poisoned my fish. And, yeah, there's a level of pettiness there that some folks would find impossible to stoop to. But not her. It had always been the tradition at Starboard Catering to hand out full turkeys to the employees on Thanksgiving and spiral hams on Christmas. Free food isn't controversial. But when Rodnicki took over, I know it was Lorraine who convinced him to stop giving the turkeys and hams away and probably skimmed the money. Maybe

Lorraine killed my fish for talking back to her the day before? Or not getting the new answering machine like I said I would?

The answering machine, which, by the way, was missing. I stood up with Curly in my hand, dripping scummy water onto my desk.

The phone rang. An internal line. Rodnicki again. I could hear Lorraine's voice in the background.

Good morning, rooster.

I slipped Curly back into his watery grave.

When I knocked on his door, Rodnicki called me in. He was calm. That perturbed me. Calm was a level of anger that was hard to integrate. In his usual bluster, Rodnicki sounded irritated with everything, but this was different. He held a sheaf of papers. Gig sheets with big red lines slashed through them. That meant cancellations. Or worse: complaints.

Lorraine leaned on the typewriter desk. I didn't look directly at her, but I knew she was staring at me. Waiting for me to slip or sneer or glance.

"Listen, McCall. I know it's a busy time, but can you find it in your fucking heart to do the job you were hired to do? I just got a call from the Chamber of Commerce saying that the chicken was roasted not fried, and that there were not enough servers on hand. Why do we not have enough people? Why am I sending out understaffed crews? They're saying they can't be sure to call us for another catering job again? They're a loyal client, McCall. Are you getting this?"

"I do. But I'm not authorized to hire, Andy. Hiring is with the Director not the Assistant Manager. And I left those applications on your desk yesterday—"

"Oh, don't, don't," Rodnicki said. He lost his mind. Spit fell into his black beard. He pounded his fist onto the desk calendar a few times. I knew everyone in the kitchen—the chefs, the bakers, the whole crew heard this. I should've been embarrassed but I wasn't. Basically, he said I didn't lose my job on a day-to-day basis because the District Manager liked me. Whatever that meant. I think he had no legit way to shitcan me. And, let's be honest—I did most of his work for him. Why would you fire someone like that? You don't. Instead, tyrants berate their captives and keep them weak.

"One last thing," he said. He pulled the answering machine from under his desk and handed it to Lorraine. It was plugged in. "Why do we still have this?"

"I meant to go yesterday—"

She cut me off by playing the message of Mr. Dinosaur's garbled voice. But this time, it was understandable, mostly. I heard that calm, breathy tone. Like he was in the room with us. Like we were coffined in the room with him. My stomach clenched. But I didn't know why. I felt exposed, as if my viscera were poking out of my belly button. Winking out like a live worm from that soft center of my guts.

"What is this? Why didn't you tell us about it?"

"No need," I said. "I followed up on it. It's crazy talk. Guy wants to eat whole camels and stuff."

Rodnicki looked disappointed. As if we'd missed out on the cooking-whole-camels angle of the catering world.

His phone rang, and I was dismissed.

On my way out, Lorraine said in a nearly audible whisper, "Sorry about your fish."

No fucking way. There was no way she could've known about Curly. She all but confirmed her guilt.

I turned to answer. Something witty. Something cutting. I wanted to scissor the smile off her face.

But two kids pushed past me into the office. One of them, a teenager, almost knocked me over. Rodnicki's kids. They sometimes ate lunch there. On whose dime? You guessed it.

Lorraine forgot about me. She was hugging and kissing her kids. Even while on the phone, Andy ruffled the young one's hair. There was a moment where I knew I hated the Rodnickis (and their dipshit kids), but I also understood why they acted the way they did. It was terrifying to be unsure about money. Even more terrifying to let someone else run you over, tell you what to do. So, in self-preservation, they did the running over first. It wasn't right, of course, but it checked out in the realm of human motivations and the drama of psychology.

All I could think was that people would be better off

separated like betta fish. If not, we'd tear each other apart.

　　　　　　　　　　※

　　Big Tiny Keller was onboard before I even finished my sentence. I didn't explain where I got the money to do the job. And when I said we'd use food from outside our inventory, he shook his biker head like I was scratching his chrome exhaust pipes.

　　"Nah. We'll use what we got in the freezers here. More than enough. That Catholic church gig fell through last week, so we need a reason to shift inventory."

　　He was right. I'd have to change the menu a bit. Glazed carrots instead of roasted asparagus. I didn't think Mr. Dinosaur or his club would care.

　　Keller sucked on a cigarette, musing.

　　"And we'll do the cooking here," he said.

　　"I think the Toothaker has a full-service kitchen."

　　"Yeah, I'm not cooking at Toothaker. I'm in to help you, but you couldn't get me to walk into that place."

　　I asked him why not.

　　"Back before it was a frat house, a few biker gangs—the Motormouths, the Dragons, the Fuck Offs—they used to party up back there in the woods. Do horrible shit to animals, women, children. To each other. Or so they say. Gives me the fantods, man. Besides, I like knowing where my own stuff is."

I had never taken Biker History 101. I wanted to know more about the "horrible" stuff.

"Alright, well. You don't think anyone will notice if we do it here?"

He shrugged. "Who cares? It's a kitchen. People cook in them. We're cooking in it. Rodnicki isn't—*hasn't*—been here that late since he took over. It'll be a breeze. In, out, done. Stick it in the hot boxes, into the chafer pans and you're on your way to self-employment."

I could not believe my dream was going to be fulfilled by a stranger over the phone with a made-up name like *Mr. Dinosaur*. I heard Keller say the word "graveyard," and I asked him to repeat what he said.

"Just this *Golden Forest* thing. My mother's grave was apparently inside this zone of explosion, one of the bodies missing, you know?"

I was horrified. He didn't seem to be.

"Hey, Cade. My ma is long dead, man. Nothing bothering her. My old man, though? He's having a time. Bunch a guys swooping in on my doorstep with paperwork and money for me not to talk. It's a pain in my ass." He leaned in and with a half-hearted conspiratorial tone said: "But let me tell you. That ain't no gas leak. They don't know what caused the explosion."

Now I was thinking how it was all this odd crap

happened in one day. But wasn't that how it went? Life trucks along quite boringly, and then *wham!*—headlong into an impossible object, hard to avoid.

"Oh, one more thing, Tiny. And it's weird. Maybe not so weird as your news." He raised his eyebrows with interest and stubbed the cig on the heel of his boot. "Do you know where I could get snake meat?"

He laughed.

"Troublemaker. I like it."

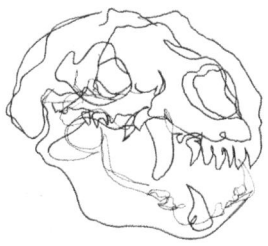

FOUR

Every employee had left for the evening, except maybe the night janitor, Randall, but he usually blew off after Rodnicki and Lorraine left. Which they did, way before everyone else. I always felt like a boss should be first in and last out, like a ship's captain.

I was finalizing menus and orders and needed to leave to oversee a big catering gig in honor of a hospital's Board of Directors. Three hundred people. I had a good crew there, but I would check on them. My desk was nearly at a condition I could walk away from when I gave a final look at Curly's small fish tank. I'd plonked his purple, scaly body into one of the toilets. I wasn't an overly sentimental soul, but that broke me a bit. A simple fish, poisoned. For what? Rage surged through me again. My wrist muscles tightened, and I stood and kicked my already broken office chair.

I heard a rattled and broken sound. I thought it was the chair. It wasn't. I held my hands out, as if that would sharpen the sound. The noise was coming from outside the manager's office. Randall often listened to WRBT on a portable radio attached to his mop cart. Probably left it on.

I realized I was stepping quietly on the tile into the kitchen. As if disturbing the static would cause it to shut off. The floors weren't wet. Not mopped. Which meant Randall took off and I was alone. I turned and walked past the prep tables and all the polished stainless steel cooking implements. The cinder block walls in there were painted an egg yolk yellow and the tile was a burnt umber. Not an appetizing combo. The mop closet was closed, and besides, the sound— which I now heard as a voice talking through static—was inside Rodnicki's office.

In disbelief, I pressed my ear against his office door. No way he was still at work. Besides, the voice was distant, like a long-haul trucker's CB squawking out a message from another trucker across the country.

I had Rodnicki's office key. Lorraine didn't know he passed me one and wouldn't have let Andy give it if she knew. But, if the boss is lazy, the second in command needs a way to cover his ass. I gently pulled the keys from my slacks' pocket. I squeezed them so they wouldn't clink. I slid the key into the deadbolt housing. Then stopped. I looked around. Why was I being so quiet? Was I acting stupid? Rodnicki had obviously left his radio on. I breathed. I knew I was being quiet because I didn't believe any of those things. Because I wanted to *hear* what was being said.

There was a bussing cart along the wall with odds and ends on it. Soup pans, tongs, long-handled metal spoons. I grabbed a spoon. It wouldn't kill anyone, but it'd hurt like a sonuvabitch on the skull.

I opened the door. A radio sat atop the file cabinet. It wasn't on. The static was clearing now. And I heard a voice, a breathy tone, as if it was right behind my ear, talking at the nape of my neck.

Hello.

Not until I saw the radio did I consciously recognize that I knew what the sound was all along. That greasy old answering machine. It was replaying the last message over and over. I opened Rodnicki's desk and found the machine in the bottom left. A little orange notification light blinked like a welcome beacon. But it was crackling away—*and* unplugged to power. My stomach grew warm with fear. Not since I was a child had I felt this kind of numbing effect spread within me. I flipped the machine over to check for batteries, but there was no slot for them. I felt like I was on the other side of a thin membrane, like the flimsy piece of plastic that wraps a single slice of cheese. And the microscopic niblet of *something* leaked through—the same feeling of my insides trying to worm their way out of my body. That cold fire from my dream returned to me. How I huddled around it in the middle of a field. How I wanted it in my belly.

The message was him. His strange message, garbled, but totally complete. Although this time, I heard something else.

> *BEEP! Hello. This is, ah, Mr. Dinosaur calling to do business. I am a member of an, ah, extreme food club and we require, ah, specific catering services. I thank you. Ahh. [phone number] BEEP!*

He called himself by the name I chose for him. How was that possible? He couldn't have known what I was drunkenly watching that night. My hands shook as I clutched this slippery machine. I pried open the top to yank out the tape. There was no tape. I took my spoon and the talking machine out of the office and to the compactor in the trash room. I tossed it in and closed the lid. The lever was massive, and it felt good to haul it down. The trash compactor geared into motion loudly, whirring and whining with compression. Cardboard, metal, plastic. Crunching and crashing together.

I visualized the answering machine being obliterated. As the crushing sounds commenced, I felt my stomach ease, the numbness wane a bit. I loosened my grip on the huge spoon and hoped to god no one would pop in through the dock doors and see me standing like an idiot ready to do battle with a pot of soup.

The compactor's green completion light blinked on and I hauled up the lever. I popped the lid and leaned my ear in again.

There. Deep in the center of that corrugated and rotten mess, in the core of that trashy funk. Right there. The weak static of Mr. Dinosaur's voice was still there—muffled and droning. And—*he just wanted our business, and, ah, he just had some specific needs.* I slammed the lid and threw the spoon. I couldn't stay and sweat over this goddamn piece of plastic. I had to get gone to the catering gig. And besides, I knew, as I got into my car, that the trash truck was going to pull up early the next morning and take the answering machine away forever. It was the smallest of consolations, and I allowed it.

But then, I'd still had the actual catering for Mr. Dinosaur. The money hugged up against my chest. More money than I'd made in one go, ever. And it could extract me from Starboard and Rodnicki, forever. I could start my own business. I'd do it better than I ever could there. I made a deal with myself: keep the engagement with Mr. Dinosaur—but bring someone I trusted as backup in case the meal went sideways.

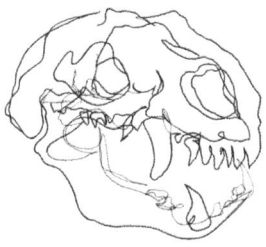

FIVE

After I returned home from the hospital gig, I flipped on all the lights in my house. The hall light from the living room to the bedroom was out. Fine. I'd survive with the others. I'd rarely been scared of the dark. But earlier at work had deeply mangled my rationality. I wanted to bring it up with the servers at the gig, like a junky asking the whereabouts of a dealer. Though, how does one introduce such weirdness?

> ME: Hey, you ever had machines that aren't plugged in talk to you?

SERVER: Yeah, lemme call the Psycho Store and get someone who can help, creepoid.

I wanted to turn on the TV for distraction but worried that PBS would air that documentary on the Cretaceous again. No thanks. I had an intentionally spare living space. A TV squatted on top of a homemade table with a recliner about six feet away. Rabbit ears reaching their skinny limbs into the aether. I fell into the chair and stared at the dead TV, drinking a beer. I didn't want to read. Didn't want to sleep. Around 2 a.m., I got restless, fed up. I thought about Mr. Dinosaur's meal. How to get through it. What to do with the eleven grand. Then images of the graveyard explosion populated my brain. I wanted to see it in person. It couldn't hurt to drive by and see what was what. Give me something to do.

Well, I was wrong. Golden Forest Cemetery was busy as hell. Police cruisers with their lightbars swirling. Strings of yellow caution tape fluttering in the wind. Pairs of idle cops chatting over coffee. Beyond this, hazmat-suited people, working in a starkly lit expanse of ground. It was like an excavation.

I laughed. The thought burbled up from my murkiest subconscious. It was like a paleontology dig. Digging for *dinosaur bones*.

Jesus.

A cop strolled to my window and knocked. I said I wanted to see what had happened. The cop bent down to get a better look at me.

"McCall?"

"Yeah?"

"It's Billy Ballantyne."

I hadn't seen Ballantyne since high school. He had been one of those people who you shared intense, formative times with, and then, sort of, fell away from after graduation. He had me get out of the car and give him a hug. We talked about life and I finally asked what the hell had happened over there. I pointed to the yellow alien suit investigators milling around, sifting dirt.

Ballantyne shrugged. "Man, they don't tell us shit. 'Just keep people out,' you know?"

"I heard it wasn't a gas leak, Billy. Work with a guy whose mom's grave was in there."

"That, my friend, you are right about. No gas leak. No explosion."

"No explosion? What the hell does all that, then?"

We moved between gravestones toward the site. His hands were hooked on his belt. The blinding white arc lights taking over the dark. We had to shield our eyes. We stood as close as we could near the edge of the impact zone.

I said it looked like a meteor strike.

"They mentioned that, too. But that's not it, either.

They don't know what it was."

"Right, but something had to have done this."

He nodded. "Yeah, *something*. But the bigger question now is: where did the bodies go?"

I stared at him.

He said that despite two full days of searching, there'd been no forensic evidence of the people who were buried in that zone. No bones, no cloth; no cement from burial crypts, no shards or fragments of caskets. Absolutely nothing but dirt upon dirt. He said that's why they were here, really. It's being treated as a crime scene. He didn't seem put out by that, or bothered. He was elsewhere.

"You remember that time I told you about camping in Labrador with my uncle and we were being followed by something," Billy said. "My uncle thought it was an irate hunter. I thought it was a bear."

"Shit yeah. I think about that all the time. You said that was the most scared you'd ever been."

Billy stepped back from the edge and walked back to his patrol car. Over his shoulder he said, "Well, this scene here is starting to edge Labrador out."

The part he didn't repeat was that they never found out what it was. Never saw what was following them. They heard it tracking them for days, morning and night.

On the way home, I found myself reciting Billy's words: *Dirt upon dirt. Dirt upon dirt. Dirt upon dirt.*

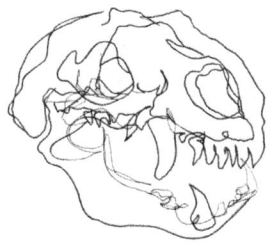

SIX

The following morning, totally butt-housed from too much beer and little sleep, I drove straight to the bank and deposited the money into my account. Even if I was being taken for a ride, I desperately wanted that fleeting feeling of possessing that much wealth for a single day.

When I pulled into the parking lot at work, something was wrong. There weren't scraps of trash by the dock. That was a sure sign of Trash Day. The big ugly truck always had a few remnants of junk escape from the back. Inside the trash room, I popped the lid again. Trash still overflowed and stank in there. But this time: no sound. Not that I could tell. I asked a few distracted chefs in the kitchen about trash pick-up. Leslie, a prep chef, said that the truck couldn't pull the compactor bin out. Got stuck. Mechanical malfunction or something. They were going to come back later in the day.

Didn't really matter, though.

I still heard that damn message in my head, *ah, thank you* my memory doing the work for the machine, *ah, do business with you.*

But it died down when I called Tina Ramsey. I wanted her to join me as server on the gig. Tina and I were almost a Thing forever and ever ago. Though that prospect was dissolving with each month. Yet we still flirted every time we were around each other. Calling each other sir and madam. She was the one employee I'd worked with who was my age. She was different. Always taking classes at the community college. A forever learner. But I couldn't ask her out. Couldn't scrounge the courage? Maybe. Mostly I didn't want to complicate shit by dating an on-again-off-again employee. Less because it was the right thing to do and more because I didn't want to bring my personal life any closer to Rodnicki and Co.

I convinced Tina pretty easily with a souped-up paycheck, of course. Twice as much as Starboard would've paid and it was under the table. Tina was the ultimate server. She was polite, knew how to tie a bowtie, had an interest in catering management, and didn't flip her wig when clients lost theirs. She'd meet me at the Toothaker to keep it quiet from Rodnicki. A light thrill remained after she accepted.

Then Big Tiny stuck his head in to report he'd sourced a snake for meat. Problem was, it was a whole snake, dead. I was disappointed. I said I was expecting sort of white chunks of flesh to deal with. But, no, this was a fang-to-tail scenario. Big Tiny Keller laughed, which was a deep *hyeugh-hyeugh*. "Hey man, free snake. Don't complain." I'd go to the library at lunch and get a book on how to dress a snake. Maybe buy that new answering machine, too.

Keller said that all of Mr. Dinosaur's menu was set aside and ready for tomorrow. He said that it would be a big help if I could break down some beef knuckles for a different gig at the same time, though. Would help him get to my food with less stress the next day. I often helped in the kitchen as necessary. There were twenty-five knuckles on a prep table. Pink, purple muscles covered in silver skin and connective tissue. I carved and cut. I pulled up the strip of tissue and slid my boning knife underneath and the flesh peeled off. I got into a system, a loop. Cut down the top, peel, skin, slice. Butterfly here. Kitchen work is a rhythm. I loved it. At about the fifteenth one, I made a cut for a piece called the bullet. It's the best part. But something caught my eye. There was silver skin on it. Or—

It was moving. Squirming. The bullet pulsed. I prodded

it with the boning knife and it stopped. I held it down, like a fish, and made a transverse incision. A bright smoke, in the shape of a string, flooded out onto the table. And afterward a pour of milky blood. I couldn't catch my breath. I felt I was falling backward. I called for Keller. When I looked up, all the knuckles had this dark, now-glittering smoke curling around them, vibrating. I yelled for Keller. Then I was just yelling. The bright smoke whipped about and tangled all together like wet shoelaces caked in mud and blood. A ball of these was forming and I stuck the boning knife into it. I couldn't help myself. It was like my hand willed it, and not my mind. But my hand got caught in the tangle. I felt one of the black strings of smoke, a sharp wire now, pierce the soft skin between my index and middle finger and shoot straight up my vein—

Then it was like emerging from dental surgery. I was in the trash room. Woozy. Standing in front of the compactor. The lid was popped open. My head was pushed over into the compacting space. I held the boning knife in one hand. In the other hand, that good piece of bullet meat.

It looked like I was trying to commit stupid suicide.

I could see in between the sour trash all the bright smoke soaking and oozing.

Keller loomed to the side of me. I felt him. He was not pleased.

"McCall, what are you doing, man? I've been looking

all over for you. You going to do these knuckles or what?"

"Huh?"

"You've done one and wasted, like, forty-five minutes. Can you help me so I can help you? Are you throwing that away? Give me that meat. That's precious, man."

He took the meat from me and returned to the kitchen.

What was I doing standing in front of an open trash compactor? For three quarters of an hour, no less. I had been blacked out, holding raw meat and a knife like a freak show. I'm lucky no one other than Keller found me. Was I trying to crush my own head? I worried about my health. I hadn't been sleeping. I'd heard that people carried out crazy actions in that liminal space between wakefulness and dreaming where the brain cranked on autopilot mode.

I finished breaking down the beef knuckles. There was no bright smoke. Then I went home and crashed. I didn't return to work. Rodnicki himself hadn't even bothered to come in. Days like that, I was ostensibly the boss. And the boss was going to sleep his nightmares off.

Twelve hours. That's how long I slept. Dreamless. Pure velvet slumber. All my lights were still burning bright, too. When I woke, I felt good, rested. I felt, well, curiously comfortable. Other than the weird shit that had been skewering me in the last few days, all of which I attributed to stress, alcohol, anxiety, lack of sleep, I felt confident. I was going to pull off this secret catering gig for a whacked-out client and I'd already banked the money. It was killer. And what if this guy wanted another meal with some other strange meat? What if he paid the same or more? It was a no-brainer. I'd do it. Whatever Mr. Dinosaur wanted, I'd get it.

All day at work, Rodnicki kept to his office. Lorraine was nowhere to be seen. Payroll was due, so it was odd she wasn't around. If checks were late (as they sometimes had been), people would revolt. When Andy Rodnicki did leave his office that day, he looked pale and sweaty like he was in eighth grade again and had forgotten to study for the math exam. He didn't bother me, and I left him alone.

After Rodnicki left for the day, Big Tiny Keller helped me transfer the food into hot boxes and we strapped them into the back of our panel van. He lit a cigarette. Smoothed his mustache.

"Godspeed, soldier. You need any help carting this crap back?"

"Tina will help." I looked forward to our one on one time.

"Gotcha."

Then he handed me the dead curled snake in a plastic

tub wrapped in Saran Wrap.

"Don't eat it all in one place."

"I won't."

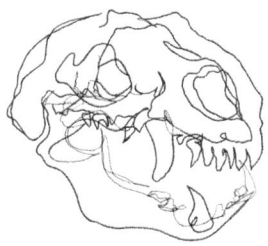

SEVEN

I arrived at the Toothaker Estate a half hour before the call sheet listed. Tina Ramsey waited in her hatchback, smoking and drinking a can of root beer. She smelled of sarsaparilla and warm tobacco. It was intoxicating.

"Hello, sir. How many?" she asked.

"Madam. Uh, the guy said nine, including himself."

She took the sheet from my hand. Our fingers touched on the sides. She smiled. She read the top of the gig sheet.

"Uhh, excuse me? 'Mr. Dinosaur'?"

"Don't ask. Not the real name. It's an extreme food

club. I got a snake back there that I gotta cut up and cook."

"What? No way!"

She thought I was nuts, but she agreed it was worth the money. She'd do the same thing. We unstrapped the food. Got it wheeled into the kitchen through the servants' entrance. The door was unlocked but took a bit of shoulder to open. I'd brought dishes, napkins, cutlery, and tablecloths. That was standard. But the Toothaker house already had good china. I figured we'd use their stuff. Looked clean.

"No tea? Coffee? No booze?" Tina asked.

I shook my head. "They said they had their own beverages."

"You ever done a gig here?"

"No. Why?"

"Smells weird. Like no one's cleaned here in a while. Look, Cade, there's mice turds on the floor there."

True story. I didn't know what to say to that. One time deal here. All I had was that money in the bank. I pretty much reminded her of the same thing. The cost/benefit ratio was in our favor. Moreover, if we got done in time, I'd take her for chess pie and weak coffee at Smitty's Diner. She got to work prepping plates, giving the cutlery a quick polish.

"You mind, good sir, if I listen to the Walkman?"

"I don't mind."

Tina set one earphone on, one off. Sounded like punk. The Ramones.

I needed to find the lights in the joint.

Two doors exited the kitchen. I chose the door to the left. The light from the kitchen shone in. It was another prep room. Storage. Tina had her back to me. Hips swaying to the rhythm. I pushed through the right, a swing door. The feeling of a great space ahead of me sunk in. You can tell how far your breath goes in pitch blackness. This was a big space. I was glad that we were here before the guests. I was meticulous, and the way we were cutting it close here didn't make me happy. The money had clouded my need to triple-check everything. To my immediate right I felt the wall. Wainscoting and textured wallpaper. No switches. The room refused to expose itself with the kitchen light. Like the darkness in that room absorbed it. It all felt like a trick. The floor creaked under my shoes as the swing door swooshed behind me. A thin line of light spread from under the door now. It didn't go far. This was the opposite of the excavation site in the graveyard. The one place I'd expect to be terrified was a graveyard at 2 a.m. But here I was at work around 8 p.m. and feeling less intrepid than ever. I set my hand on the wall and felt slowly over to the left side along the wainscoting. My other hand was slightly above that. I took a step and stopped.

That lizard brain warning system that another physical shape is in your vicinity flared off. And I heard breathing. *Something* like it. Not my own, but another person in the room.

Not far behind me. I cleared my throat too loudly (something I did from childhood when walking down a dark hallway—as if monsters and ghosts were polite and understood the inconvenience of mauling me). I shifted my feet/stomped on the floorboard to get Tina's attention. That is, if the music hit that brief nothing that exists between songs. Tina called it the Nothing That Is. An eternal pause, a place of safety before the chaos of guitar and drums. She said she sometimes cherished that moment more than anything. I was in some sense cherishing my moment here. I rushed along the last foot until I was halted by the switches. One of them stabbed me in the soft flesh between the index and middle finger. The sense memory bit like a dog. I wanted to live in the pause. In pain, I flipped the switch.

A man sat behind me. He was in a wingback chair at the head of a long dining table under a strange sheet. There was a golden ring around his head to hold the sheet and there were spaces for his eyes and a flap for his mouth when he ate. I had a brief thought that *this was made from the same thing as the bright smoke and cold fire.*

He was staring straight ahead.

His eyes were wide open.

I slipped but caught myself. The man didn't turn his head or give any notion that he knew I was there. Not at first. I tried to talk but I couldn't think of anything to say. Sorry? For what?

I mean, I knew who this was. I had never been more certain of a person's identity in my life.

Mr. Dinosaur sat as if he'd been there forty thousand years.

It was at that moment, when I clocked who he was, that he turned to me. As if some ancient mechanism in his chest sputtered to life, giving spark to the animatronics. The sheet disturbed me. But then, there was all the money he'd paid me. Hard to ignore.

"Hello, Mr. McCall. You're, ah, early. I apologize for not turning the lights, ah, on."

"That's okay. We're setting up in the kitchen. I'm sorry, but for formality's sake, you are the man I spoke with on the phone? Correct?"

He nodded. "Mr. Dinosaur, yes. You received your money."

"I did, thank you. Will you be wearing that sheet all night? Is this a ceremony?"

Mr. Dinosaur didn't respond. I didn't want to offend, but I also wanted to know. I erred on not knowing for now.

With this small crust of civility in place, I noticed he was alone. Other than the wingback and the table he sat at, the rest of the furniture in the large dining area was shabby with age. Clearly everything had been neglected for years. Tina was right. The dining room, like the rest of the Toothaker Estate, was musty and stale.

"I thought you were part of an extreme food club?"

"True."

"Where's everyone else?"

"They could not make it."

"Excuse me?"

"They could not make it, Mr. McCall. I am your only diner tonight."

I laughed too loudly then, at the absurdity of it all. I realized what was going on. I was getting tricked, pranked. Andy and Lorraine Rodnicki had set this whole goddamn farce up. They found some guy to call and leave a weird message and, of course, Lorraine could swap the tape after taking the answering machine. Probably had someone wire it so it would repeat the same weird phrase over and over. To add misery, she killed my fish. They knew I knew about their embezzlement. The eleven thousand in my bank account was probably money they'd stolen, getting funneled to me so I would look guilty as shit. I was getting set-up to take the motherfucking fall for them. Insane.

I leaned forward on the table and looked into this guy's eyes. Or as best as I could look into those darkened portals.

"How long has Rodnicki been planning this?"

"Pardon."

"Andy Rodnicki. Or his wife, Lorraine. Did she set this up? You know what they're doing, right?"

"I am afraid I have no idea what you are talking about."

"Hmm."

A dish broke in the kitchen. Not ours. I could tell. Which meant it was an expensive dish. Dammit, Tina. I yelled if everything was alright. Tina called back, "Yeah, salad plate. Sorry."

"Mr. McCall, would you be so kind as to hear a few more requests of mine before we begin service?"

It was hard for me to lift my hands off the table. I wanted to press on with my point, but I gave in.

"Sure."

"Thank you, ah, I have some rules. The first is that you are the only person to go between the kitchen and this dining room. Your colleague must never enter here. Second, I am as you see me. I will not move. I will kindly ask that you assist in helping feed me my meal."

"Are you saying you're handicapped and need my help to eat?"

"No, not handicapped. I wish your help in eating."

"Mr.—"

"*Dinosaur*," he said.

"Mr. Dinosaur, this wasn't part of the service. And, anyway, Starboard Catering doesn't feel equipped or like we're the appropriate business to—"

"Enough, Mr. McCall. Did I pay you before services rendered for eleven thousand dollars?"

I said he did.

"Then I would like you to feed me the food I purchased, and which is slowly growing cold in that kitchen beyond. Can you abide by my rules?"

The cloth near his mouth fluttered.

I nodded. *The money the money the money.*

"And were you able to bring the extra item?"

"I was able to get a snake for you, yes. But the bad news is no one in my kitchen, none of my chefs, are familiar with dressing or preparing snake meat."

Mr. Dinosaur...shrugged?

"That is of no mind now. We shall get to it soon enough. You may proceed with the first course when you are ready."

He kept his head forward as if he was at the helm of some great and vast ship. Some vessel which only he could see and I was oblivious to. I walked backward to the swing door and caught Tina before she was coming out.

"You can't go in there."

She pulled her headphones down. "Huh? What are you talking about? How am I going to do my job?"

"How about I pay you to stay in here?"

"Fuck you, Cade." She laughed. "I mean, sir."

"Seriously. Mr. Dinosaur is in there. He's already been here. Like, maybe, for hours, waiting in the dark. He wants only one server."

"Liar."

"Scout's honor."

"This is messed up, man. This is some misogynist shit."

"*Tina.*"

"Kidding." She wasn't. Now I distinctly heard Wall of Voodoo from her headphones. "I want an extra hundred."

"Deal."

"Alright. What should I do? Nine plates—"

"Um, just one. He's the only one apparently. Everyone else canceled."

Tina held a dinner plate to her chest like a textbook.

"Cade. Sweetie. I know I need money bad, like bananas bad. But this? This Addams Family on crack shit I do not need. Nor do you." She tried to see past my shoulder. She touched my cheek and her hand was warm. One time, she and I drove four hours to see a Mission of Burma show in Columbus, Ohio. She playfully held my hand in the car the way there. And during the show, she slammed her body into mine. Driving back, she slumped over on me, sleeping. I couldn't stop thinking of that. "I mean this: let's go. Leave this shit here. Get it tomorrow. Let's roll."

She put the plate down and headed for the door. I didn't want to say this but—

"You leave, you miss that extra hundred."

"No one needs a hundred this bad," she said, dismissive. "But you are paying me every penny you promised for this gig."

She was disappointed but knew I would follow through.

The music from her headphones sounded delicious. Faraway. She put on her jacket and headed out the door. She caught herself by the fingertips and swung back and said, "You're sure this isn't a prank? Like Big Tiny or somebody?"

"Is it?" I asked. If there was a moment when the reveal would happen, I figured now would be it.

She shrugged. Said no. She blew a cartoony kiss and jogged down the driveway to her car. It rumbled and the lights swept through the kitchen and off she went.

In that moment, I felt as if I'd been left on the Moon by my fellow astronauts for years to come. *And that I'd requested it.* This was the most stranded a human could be in—on—the earth itself. Of that, I had zero doubt. And the silence. Much like the silence she'd described between songs on a tape. The nothing that is. It was hard to enjoy, to revel in.

I plated the food he ordered. Meat, veg, starch, an onion roll. I folded a napkin, and brought a fork, knife, and spoon. As I moved to press my back into the swing door, I could see my reflection in the glass panel of the rear exit door. This meal will not end with this plate of food, I thought. Or the snake.

First, there was a salad. He was particular. Mr. Dinosaur must've had his hands placed palms down on the table under the sheet. I could only recognize shapes underneath it. He didn't move his torso. I had to lift the cloth flap to feed the food in. The spoon always came out clean. And dry, as if he had no saliva. I heard nor saw a jaw chew the food. It was like dropping stuff off a cliff into the sea.

I had a new theory. I wondered, as I fed him in silence, if this guy wasn't some incredibly rich weirdo who had no friends and pulled stunts like this to enjoy human interaction. The money explained it. The oddness was there.

I said I was sorry that his friends canceled on such short notice.

He did not answer.

I said it must be hard to have an Extreme Food Club in such a small Midwestern town. "Not a lot of experimental foods to try."

"It is not hard to find victuals outside the usual range."

I stopped. A piece of carrot speared on the end of the fork.

"Excuse me? *Victuals?*"

"Yes, food. I have no problem eating strange foods."

"I bet. You seem resourceful."

"I have my ways, Mr. McCall."

I was too embarrassed to bring up my new theory. In light of the way I'd accused him about knowing Rodnicki, it seemed dumb. Also, I wanted to leave. I felt like less and less light was coming from the wall sconces and the chandelier overhead. And that the longer I stood next to Mr. Dinosaur, the harder it was to pull myself away. Literally. I felt drawn to him. Even a small jaunt into the kitchen to get salt hurt until

I returned to him.

We finished the salad and main course. He stared straight ahead.

"May I ask a question, Mr. Dinosaur."

"You may."

"Are you—I am sorry to ask this so brazenly—are you able to walk?"

He turned his head to look at me. But the way he did it was as if an unseen hand was pushing his chin toward me. The weird sheet didn't rumple like cloth should.

"I can walk, ah, but in this *eon* I am, ah, limited for a time."

"Oh, okay."

I didn't know what to do with that answer.

"So, if you don't mind me asking, what's your real name?"

The unseen hand pushed his chin away from me.

Mr. Dinosaur didn't answer. I know he heard me.

"Mr. McCall, I believe it is time for the snake."

I cleared the setting and brought in the plastic tub with the snake. I showed it to him like it was a bottle of expensive wine he'd ordered.

"I have to apologize for not knowing—"

"Please, take it out."

Snakes aren't everyday handling for me. I wanted gloves. But, again, I thought: if it's dead, then who cares?

"How would you like me to prepare this? Or, how do you prepare this? To be honest with you, I was only able to get this at the last minute, and that's because you paid so much for the service."

"I understand," Mr. Dinosaur said. "Open the snake's mouth, Mr. McCall, place your finger down the throat, and pull away."

"Rip it apart?"

"In effect, yes."

Calculating risk is a funny thing. I don't think I ever was good at it. I asked myself: is it quicker to go through this or resist it? I uncurled the snake, which felt like a cold, dry coil of wire. I wedged open its mouth, careful of fangs. The feeling of its mouth was only odd because of what it was. I'd had my hand in some gruesome shit. One time, at work, a chef left a large sink full of turkeys to defrost with water dripping over them. The chef forgot them. So I had to press my hand into the mush up to my elbow to get at the drain and clear it. A finger down a snake mouth wasn't much. It was like tearing a wet bedsheet. Took a few goes to get an opening. Then I finally pulled, yanked, and the innards hung in a line and blood flung out. Some got on Mr. Dinosaur's sheet. I apologized. He seemed thrilled.

I had to look away. My mouth was getting that saliva build up that occurs right before puking. That tart strike of nerves along the jawline.

"Now what?" I choked out.

"Now push the snake down my throat," Mr. Dinosaur said.

I heard this clearly.

"No. I will not. This is insane. I've gone this far with you, but I'm not shoving a snake down your throat. I think we need to end it here." I threw down the snake. "Is there someone I need to call and come get you?" My red-drenched hands hung at my sides like gore mittens.

If there was a way he could've gone more still and rigid, he did. Almost like his hands sank *into* the surface of the table.

"My guests have decided to show after all," he said.

"What?"

I didn't hear anything. But then above us, on the second floor, a soft galloping like a cat shooting from one side of a room to the other. And outside the front of the Toothaker house, I heard the *shuff* of what sounded like a large tree falling.

"I'll have to ask you to leave the room, Mr. McCall. If you would wait in the kitchen until this is over."

What was "this"?

"Please," he insisted.

Before I backed into the swing door, I looked real quick. Under the sheet, Mr. Dinosaur's head was tilted back, and the mouth was open. Far too wide for any person to endure.

The skin around the mouth seemed distended and bloodless, almost gray white. No vasculature to speak of below it. His lips had turned black. There was no struggle from him. He welcomed it. The guts of the poor ripped snake were piled on the table before him, and I felt hot tears pricking at the corners of my eyes—I hated hurting anything. Why did I do this? Why did I treat Tina that way, so abrupt?

In the kitchen, I skidded to the back door and locked it. As if a deadbolt would keep anything out. I cupped my hands and pressed my face to the glass to cut the glare. Blackness outside. Not even a sodium light in the parking area. No back door light. I hadn't noticed that when we unloaded. The panel truck was still parked close by. Wind brushed the trees' leaves like hair.

An immense gasp came from the dining room, a dramatic in-suck of air. I felt the draw and breeze of it past my ankles. Instinct was to go in. But I caught myself. Instead, I grabbed a large metal serving spoon and used the reflection in it to see what was happening.

I held the spoon convex side toward me and pulled the door ever so slightly open. The story of Perseus hurled itself into my memory. We read it in high school. He used a reflective surface to glimpse Medusa and her head of serpentine hair from around a corner. My spoon wasn't a mirror. It was blurry. I could make out general shapes. Light sources. From what I could tell, Mr. Dinosaur sat in the same position. There was movement, though, mostly around his face, something whipping around. I couldn't be sure.

It didn't look like he was alone, though. Or, maybe his hands *did* work, and he was flailing them around now, the sheet flapping about. He gurgled. It sounded like a football team making friends with a free buffet after practicing drills. Or a pig farm at the trough. While I tried to discern what was going on in the dining room, my imagination sprinted ahead of me. I was picturing in my head small hands reaching out of his mouth. Minuscule and pale gray, these hands would grip Mr. Dinosaur's bottom lip and pull whatever it was up and out—and they'd be smaller versions of Mr. Dinosaur, maybe four inches tall. (I saw this quite clearly in my head.) They would fall out of the mouth slowly slowly, so slowly, and onto the table. The first wouldn't recover until the second one climbed its way out and in a graceful and excruciatingly slow fall, *flumph'd* onto the table next to it. I didn't see this in the spoon, obviously. But I couldn't unsee it in my head. I felt like I'd fallen behind the couch of reality and was, as I said, forgotten by everyone. Left to witness this fucktastic dreamscape.

I wanted to run. Leave it all behind. I would've given all the money away to orphans or D.A.R.E. or the Ronald McDonald House. Whatever. Just get everything about Mr. Dinosaur away from me. Why did I not listen to Tina?

I kept staring into the back of this spoon, trying to

decipher the broad movement and gelatinous sounds. One time I'd dropped a sheet pan of Jell-O onto the kitchen floor at Starboard. What was going on in the other room sounded much like that. I was worried Mr. Dinosaur's gaze would fall my way, checking on the door to make sure I wasn't peeking. But whatever he was going through was fully devotional and unwavering. I polished the spoon on my slacks. Anything to help see more clearly (though I didn't want to). When I angled the spoon back near the opening, something was behind Mr. Dinosaur as the sounds died down—it was a shape, like a shadow made solid or it could've been someone dressed in black, but this thing didn't have a human outline. It stood behind Mr. Dinosaur. Then, even though it had no face or eyes, and it was a lump of confusion in this reflective spoon, this hillbilly Perseus Shield-of-Stupid: *I knew this thing had brought its attention to bear on me.*

The black shape knew I'd seen it.

I let go of the door and turned the kitchen lights back on. I did not let go of the spoon. I waited. I was sweating all over. My palms stung, my feet slid in my socks and shoes. That space between my ass and balls was swampy and I needed to both shit and piss but knew that my muscles were way too locked up to let anything out. Those sounds in the dining room were now, well, non-existent. Silence. All I wanted was a phone. But the kitchen didn't have one—not one in sight, anyway. I'd call Billy Ballantyne. Or Big Tiny. As much as I'd wanted Tina, I couldn't re-draw her into this mess.

God. Tina knew what was up. Good girl. Got the jeff outta Dodge. Good work.

Finally, as if he was directly on the other side of the swing door, Mr. Dinosaur said, "Mr. McCall, enter."

I pushed the door open and Mr. Dinosaur was still in the flowery wingback chair under his uncanny sheet, but now the room was a total disaster and blood had been flung and splattered everywhere like a demonic abstract expressionist painting.

"If you leave now, Mr. McCall, that money you deposited will not be there tomorrow morning. If you help me with one more item, I can double the current amount we agreed on."

Money. Always goddamn money.

But. Consider this. Twenty-two thousand dollars would allow me total freedom from Starboard Catering Services *forever*. I could leave all the supplies at the Toothaker even. Make the next assistant manager sucker come retrieve it. It was an amount I could use to leave the Midwest and start a business elsewhere, far from Rodnicki, and now, far from Mr. Dinosaur.

The sheet he was under had like wet spots on it, or places where it was soaked. I crossed my arms with the spoon still clenched in my fist. I looked like a failed Arthurian crusader. The milksop who thought he could fight.

"What do you want?" I asked.

He was amused.

"Oh, I want, ah, *everything*, eventually. But right now, let's start with that spoon."

For some reason, I craved possession of the spoon. It was an information gatherer and a weapon (no, it wasn't—but cowards will have their shields). I felt we'd both been through something together. I glanced down at it and thought the black shape was still reflected there, but I was wrong.

"If I give you this, are we done? Money's given, I clean up and go? Over, right?"

"Sure."

The room smelled deeply aquatic, like an unclean fish tank. Overrun with algae. And over top of that was the high alkaline stench of something faintly bleachy, like semen. It was difficult to breathe through my nose.

I handed over the spoon.

"No, no. I want to eat it. Feed it to me."

I sighed. I closed my eyes and tightened my grip on the spoon. The thought emerged that I should brain Mr. Dinosaur, bash the front end of whatever skull was in there like a soft-boiled egg. But my luck running as it had been, I'd crack the bastard's lid open and a viscous evil fluid would leak out and corrode the floor and table as fast as rain ate snow.

"Which end first?" I asked.

"As it suits you."

I clambered onto the table and stood above Mr. Dinosaur. Even in this position, I felt his command of the room. His mouth-opening flap was wide enough the serving spoon could slide down without touching his cheeks or teeth. I could see nothing there. It was like looking out the back window of the kitchen, how, at first, your eyes had to adjust and you saw purely nothing. That was down Mr. Dinosaur's throat. I did not want to touch this person/thing's body, yet I had to. Apologizing, as I steadied Mr. Dinosaur's "jaw" with one hand, I pressed the end of the spoon into the darkness. His sheet was clammy and greasy like the answering machine button. But more accurately, it was like holding a room temp piece of salami. There was resistance, despite there not being anything there. It was like pushing a wad hair through a sink pipe. Shove. Shove. Inching it along, slowly, slowly. Then, the spoon got stuck. I tried to push/pull on my end, but it was like something had clutched the other end and tugged. I could feel Mr. Dinosaur's gaze on me through the sheet. Calm as a calf in a field on a summer day.

Hooks. That was the word piercing my consciousness. It seemed like there were hooks reticulating inside Mr. Dinosaur's throat. But it was so hard to see. Something was tugging the spoon downward. Finally, I let go.

Peristalsis is the involuntary act of your esophagus squeezing partially chewed food into the stomach. This was the nightmare version of peristalsis. I collapsed backward onto the table. The metal spoon wobbled and sank down inside him like an old iron ship into the sea.

"Do not worry, Mr. McCall. I have durable teeth. I come from a long line of durable teeth."

"I bet you do," I said, sliding off the table. "So now what? Is that it?"

"For now."

"Are you going to sit here?"

"That bothers you?"

"Yes. I brought a woman with me and food for nine people. I found a *snake* for you. And I did all this. I fed you, pulled apart that poor animal and shoved a metal object into your body—which I am sure no doctor would recommend. I'm a bit put off."

"Your other money is in your account. You can check to confirm."

"Don't call me again. I'm not doing business with you."

"Oh, Mr. McCall, I have, ah, so much more to eat."

"Well, I won't be the one feeding you."

"I think you shall." His answer was so sure, as if he'd already asked me in another dimension, and I'd said yes. The confidence drove anger in me as much as anxiety. His hands still rested, I imagined, heavy as decorative stone lions in front of mansions. "People just, ah, consume things, do they not? They do not, ah, really *taste* what they eat. Imagine how different it would be if people actually *tasted everything*."

"Tasting everything sounds like a horrible prospect."

"Maybe to someone with a narrow-enough mind, perhaps."

The sheet stared at me. And, in a sparked vision, I "knew" what Mr. Dinosaur did. I saw him—it—eating the history of a person from dead body backwards—and the necessity of taking a pseudo-human form meant he needed bounded help: me.

A hard knocking came at the back kitchen door. A frantic human knocking. Like a father who'd lost his son after dark, canvassing the neighborhood. Wiping what I could onto my slacks, I headed into the kitchen. Mr. Dinosaur said, "Good-bye now," and the phrase had so little finality in it, that my arms shook in that primal fear.

Big Tiny Keller was standing on the other side of the door, looking like that frantic father, and I was that lost son. He was scared, relieved, and disappointed. I could see he was trying to tell what had been going on in the past hour or two. I didn't want him here. I didn't want to be there myself. I made a hand motion to be quiet and that I would open the door slowly. I cracked it open, and the air that poured in was balmy, refreshing. It smelled like vegetation and something like bread.

"What are you doing here? You should go."

"Let me in," Keller said. Funny thing was: if he wanted

in, he could've gotten in. He was being overly polite. Letting me know that he still respected a sliver of my employer authority. Which was sweet but misguided, in hindsight. "Whatever you're doing, stop and let's go. I'll come back and get this shit later."

"I appreciate the concern, and I agree with you, but the situation here is—"

Big Tiny Keller threw all his weight behind his side. I set my feet like a police lock. But his strength gave me little ability to stop him. I slid with the door backward to the wall.

"Okay fine," I said, giving up, "but don't go in there."

Keller stepped past me and reached out to touch the swing door. I made an animalistic crowing sound, which was louder than I expected. I had a vision of a swollen and enlarged Mr. Dinosaur bending down and snapping Keller's head off, swallowing it whole. Or that fuzzy shape I saw reflected in the spoon, that *thing* would merely envelope him and then take me, or not. I didn't know which would've been worse if it had come to pass.

But Keller swung it open and held it as he surveyed the dining room. I held my breath waiting for Mr. Dinosaur's welcome. I scrambled up to explain.

"What in the actual hell is this?" Keller said.

"He doesn't want to be bothered."

"Who?"

I squeezed behind him and found—nothing. No Mr.

Dinosaur, no flowery wingback. There was a solid fucked up mess all over. The snake Keller got me, torn apart and eviscerated, the innards of it flung everywhere. I noticed some on the chandelier now. And a thin, gray, gruelish liquid in small puddles and streaks across the dining table and floor where Mr. Dinosaur had sat.

"He was there, right there in a chair. He didn't move the whole time. He had me feed him, and I didn't want to, but then, the money..."

"Stop," Keller said. "Let's say I believe whatever you're about to say."

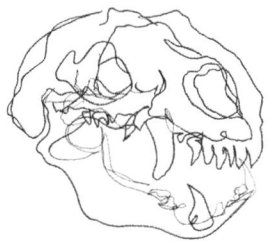

EIGHT

Big Tiny Keller said he called a biker buddy of his and this guy confirmed that, yeah, he'd heard weird shit went down here many years ago. Never saw it himself, but heard plenty about it. Keller then also tried to call the Toothaker Estate to catch me from carrying out the gig but there's no phone number for the place. Moreover, no phone. When Keller found out who the owner was, he called her. An older woman, a Mrs. Whitlow, who owned lots of properties in the county. He asked if she would ever rent the house out. Not if she *had*. She said she never rented it out for anything.

"You think I'm goddamn certified, don't you, Tiny?"

I felt his hand on my shoulder. "Aww, hell no, man. Listen, let's you and me clean this up real fast and get the hell out of here. We'll talk about it elsewhere." He sniffed the air. "Smells funky in here."

Keller helped me clean. He had to get on top of the table and raise me up to clean the chandelier. As I plucked gobbets of snake off, he said never to accept a job like this again. Definitely not over the phone. I didn't have the heart to say that it might've been too late to not accept another job with Mr. Dinosaur. Although I hadn't accepted, I felt as if my even showing up that night was an acknowledgement of perpetual complicity. Items were missing or gone, besides the client and his chair. Furniture under drop cloths, part of the wainscoting, the switch plate cover, a painting on the far side of the room. All of it gone, as if sucked up by a vacuum.

We stood out by the panel van, in the night, and I was feeling licked clean by the outside. Keller smoked and assessed me, as if I was a bomb that needed defused, though he wasn't sure which wire to cut first.

"You wanna tell me about what went down in there?"

"No, not right now."

He threw his hands up as if to say *not offended at all*.

I asked if I could talk to the biker he called, and Keller corrected himself that it was the widow of the biker he knew—because really all the biker gangs have disappeared or vanished or were presumed dead—the Dragons, the Motormouths, and the Fuck Offs. None left.

"Oh."

Keller suggested that some of this was an act on my part, a monumental reaction to stress from the Rodnickis and what was assuredly a soon-to-fail embezzlement scheme by them. And on the back of our hard work.

"I mean, like I said, assume I believe you about this Mr. Dinosaur guy, and he split before I got here. Fine. But there's still money. That money you got, that's real, right? I don't want it to be a problem for you. I got a call from someone tonight, Cade, asking about you and Andy."

"Who was it?"

"Some investigator Starboard Catering hired. Name's Chessman. He's looking into the skimming and all that. He was asking questions about you, if you're trustworthy, how much contact you have with money, do you have any money problems, any sick relatives."

My stomach turned. This guy was trying to pin embezzlement on me? I had a queasy feeling that the Rodnickis would slink out of this somehow and leave me holding the bag. I returned, albeit for a brief moment, to my theory about Mr. Dinosaur as a ploy by Andy and Lorraine. But while they were slick enough to skim cash, they weren't this sophisticated or creative. No, Mr. Dinosaur was his own thing. And now I also had this. Keller saw my worry and threw down his cigarette.

"Don't worry. I told him you're clean. You're the one keeping us afloat. I gave my two cents on the Rodnickis and it wasn't kind. How about that? Now, when this all clears over, you still going to leave Starboard?"

If the money was real, yes. If the money had truly been doubled (I knew it was) then, yes.

I nodded. I had no energy for words.

"Then I'm still with you, man. I'll leave those dicks in a heartbeat. Just say the word."

I thanked Big Tiny Keller. He gave me a guy hug, which was a punch in the clavicle. Then he told me to go home and go the fuck to bed.

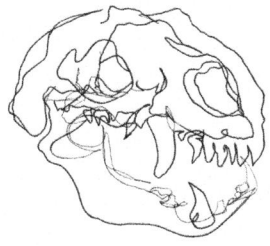

NINE

On the way back into town, chugging along in the van, sweating and trying to manage the recent itchy dump of adrenaline in my bloodstream, I noticed a local rural landmark, a stand of three corn silos, was completely dark. I could barely make out the vast metallic outline of them as I passed. They always had these big dramatic lights hanging from the sides to guide the farm trucks at night during harvest season. Strange that it was dark. But, then, edging into town, big swathes of neighborhoods' and businesses' lights had winked out. My scalp tingled. That adrenaline started leaking back in again. What the hell was going on? I turned on the radio. After a commercial, the news announced that the excavation at the graveyard was taking up power and a surge there tripped the local electrical stations. Crews were on the way, and power was expected to be restored in the next hour or so.

A clip from earlier in the day ran. It was an interview with a state analyst at the scene and the confusion now was: where did all the dirt go? None of it scattered up and out as you would expect with an explosion or impact. "It seems that everything that had been there," the analyst said, "is now suddenly gone, missing." The story concluded with a small clip about how the families of those who were buried in the Missing Zone were filing lawsuits and expecting more from the cemetery and state. So far, it seemed as if zero answers would be coming.

I sympathized. But I knew where they'd gone.

I dropped the truck off at work, but couldn't bring myself to unload it, even though Starboard's lights were one of the few places that hadn't gone out. I just wanted to go home. The trash truck must've gotten the compactor unstuck. A swirl of paper was skipping around the dock under the orange security lights.

That was the overriding color of the world that night as I found my way home. A pale but bright orangish color of streetlamps and security lights. My own car's headlights, a trusty but coughing 1979 Toyota Corolla, cut the orange with a white knife. I drove slowly. I both wanted to be home now, and not. Movement seemed safe. If I wasn't stopped in one spot, I couldn't be located by Mr. Dinosaur, or anyone. The window was down a bit and I heard the hum of tires, but nothing else. And I peered into the front windows of passing homes, trying to discern what the hell was happening in each one. But the more blacked out houses I passed, the more nervous I became. I had jolting visions of Mr. Dinosaur in his wingback chair, arms resting, these unwary sleepers with their feet in his mouth, and his teeth grinding and chewing and pulling the doomed folks down into that void I pushed the spoon into.

How does one purge nightmares? Or can they be extinguished? Maybe they're like an eternal flame, the kind that was supposedly the cause of the graveyard explosion?

Bullshit. All of it.

Then, in a bottoming out of courage, I drove past Smitty's Diner. This was where I should've been. Eating, laughing. I slowed in the street and pulled to the curb, let the engine idle. I stared at the diner, and the inside of my body shivered like when I would rise in the night to piss and all that once-welcomed heat flowed out of me. I was drained in the car. Somehow Smitty's Diner represented stability in the town to me, especially since it was a twenty-four hour joint. But now the small diner with wrap-around glass windows and a long mica-topped counter was dead in the dark. There were cars in the parking lot. But no one in the diner. I could see abandoned coffee cups and plates of flapjacks. Brown plastic pebbled glasses of water. The orange streetlamp above me fizzled, fluttered. I pulled from the curb and went home.

My apartment building's lights were totally out. I took my flashlight from the glove compartment. I had expected this, it was fine. I tried to be as quiet as possible, because I wanted to hear what was going on behind my neighbors' doors—yet even though I was tiptoeing, I heard nothing. No one seemed up, awake, milling. No snoring, no telephones, no nothing. But as I turned out of the staircase into my hallway, I noticed the only door with a blue glow coming from the tiny crack in the hinge. The blue glow of my TV. There was, distantly, a chance that I'd left it on myself. There was also a chance that I'd forgotten to lock the door and a neighbor kid was in there watching the tube. Why was my place the only one with power, though? After seeing Smitty's lights all burned out, something about the cool glow of the television from my own place lured me. I felt driven, in a way. And when I stuck the key in the door, I knew I wanted to see what was on the other side.

 Holding the edge of my door, I pushed it open quietly and heard the murmur of the TV. I stood in the threshold. My recliner was gone. It had been replaced. There in the middle of my living room was Mr. Dinosaur's wingback. It was hard for me to lift a foot. I left the key in the door lock. I walked toward the wingback with its flowing, flowery designs in raised embroidery. The sides kept me from seeing if anyone sat in the chair. It seemed as if the chair itself was watching television, the angle in which it was arranged. And it had a sense of intent and attention coming from it. I don't know how I sensed that, but I knew the chair was aware of my presence. I stopped. I knew I didn't have it in me to look around the side of the chair and see who was in it. I kneeled to look under the chair, see if any legs touched the floor. None did. Questions like: *how did it get into my apartment?* were rather moot at this point. And I knew who was responsible for this. The wingback looked so out of place in my apartment. It belonged in a dusty corner of an old library or an aging socialite's home.

I did not want to speak. I would've been pleased just crouching there all night. I felt I could've fallen asleep in that pose. Still, I swallowed as much saliva as I could to wet my throat and spoke.

"Hello? Who's there?"

A dirt and alkaline smell rose from the floor. From the chair—whether on the other side, or from inside it. I felt unstable not knowing where to pinpoint its source. That burning adrenaline feeling shattered my veins again. I was on the verge of collapse.

I may've been crying. I had salt in my mouth, on my lips. My eyes and nose burned with acrid sharpness.

"You said you'd leave me alone! I fed you. Leave me alone!"

Disappointment radiated from the wingback. Distortion. Deterioration. Decay.

I was desperate, exhausted. I had nowhere else to go mentally. I opened a drawer in my kitchen, pulled out a chef's knife, and ran up to the chair, stabbing it in the back. Over and over. Grunting and coughing. I whipped the chair around to see Mr. Dinosaur, but the chair was empty. Right then, the lights blinked on in my apartment. The TV was at a dull roar. I assumed that power was restored over the entire town. Bolstered by the sudden light all around, I picked up the wingback, or tried, and dragged it into the hallway, where I dumped it. I shut and locked the door.

I would not let go of the knife until morning. I opened a beer and stood drinking it when I noticed the MESSAGE light notifying me on the answering machine that the day was not done with me. Part of me said, let it go, but the other part said that if it was Mr. Dinosaur, I wanted to know what he said.

Instead, it was that independent investigator hired by Starboard Catering who was looking into potential fraud and embezzlement. I was asked to contact this guy, Mr. Chessman. Also, I was to keep the investigation private. Mr.

Chessman said he'd show up at work around lunchtime for a short talk.

It spoke to my warped sense of reality that I now welcomed a fraud investigation—one that would likely and falsely implicate me—to the events that revolved in my mind.

I finally noticed what the wingback had been watching. It was the same PBS documentary about the Cretaceous.

Good god.

I started this whole thing. I called him.

As I watched the documentary more closely this time, I grew terrified of the prospect, or fact, of actual dinosaurs. They had lived so long ago and for so long. Hundreds of millions of years. It was staggering. Whereas humans had only been around a blip of a fraction of that time. What, one hundred thousand years? A little more? Moreover, dinosaurs I'd always associated with each other as a boy were apparently eons apart in time, like the brontosaur and the tyrannosaur or the triceratops. The latter two were in a whole other era of time than the former. What the hell? My mind could not correlate everything that'd gone on that day, and trying to slather a layer of time icing over it wasn't doing me any favors.

I must've fallen asleep in front of the TV and crawled to bed at some point. All with the knife in my hand. After a while, I woke to a rapid screeching and a hoof-like dancing on the other side of my walls. A vision violated my mindscape:

Mr. Dinosaur crawling rapidly and predatorily all around my hallway like an ant stuck in a paper tube. A few times through the night, there was a knocking at my door. Soft, gentle. I wanted it to be Tina. Oh, did I. She'd come in, we'd hold each other, she'd play a tape of punk music. We'd kiss each other and maybe get sweaty. But no.

I knew it was the wingback.

A roving, maniacal, and unmerciful seat.

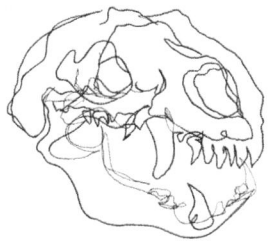

TEN

In the morning, the wingback was gone. I had opened the door with my knife in my hand, expecting to battle with it, but instead I scared the eighth grader who lived next door and was trudging to school.

"Hi, Tracy."

I waggled the knife in hello, looking up and down the hallway.

"Uh, hi, Cade."

She bolted down the hall and the stairs.

Before I went to work, I stopped by the bank and got

an account summary. The teller was a woman I'd flirted with every time I came in. She'd goof with me, flirt back. It was a contextual thing, because this time she noticed my frantic and sweaty demeanor. She asked if I was okay as she printed my summary slip. "Chronic nightmares," I said. "Not a lot of sleep." She stuck her lip out and tilted her head as if to a puppy with mange. "Poor thing." I couldn't tell if she was being facetious or not. The slip said I had a little over twenty-two thousand dollars. I tried not to hyperventilate. Immediately, I wanted to quit Starboard and move. Move out of town, out of state. Hell, maybe even the country. All I needed was my car. Maybe I'd snag Curly's old fish tank and the picture of Elly Mae Clampett. Then I decided, no, I would take nothing. I knew a friend in Maine who worked on an allotment and took care of goats—

But just as fast as I decided to flee, a cement-heavy feeling of dread flushed my bowels and into my legs. I knew I wasn't going anywhere. I knew that I would drive to work and sit at that godforsaken desk and sort, correct, and approve menus.

At work, the panel truck had already been unloaded, I assumed by Keller. I found him, thanked him, paid him. He said, "Chessman was in here this morning, asking for you. Everything cool?"

I said it was.

"I heard what was going on at the cemetery, Tiny. I'm

really sorry, man. If there's anything I can do for you..."

"You can stop the kids in my dad's neighborhood from playing ding-dong ditch. He's constantly bothered by them all hours of the night. He's been pretty fragile since mom died, so that's where I am right now."

Hmm. Could've been that the cautious knocking at my door and the running around in the hallway were kids acting up. Though I doubted it. Then I wondered if it was really kids who were bothering Tiny's dad. I couldn't get into that just then.

Work was normal. I adjusted the schedules for the few floor managers under me, did monthly inventory numbers, and helped make a huge batch of mashed potatoes for a four hundred person gig. It was nearly after lunch when the "official looking guy" found me breaking down a few boxes outside on the dock. His full name was Kurt Chessman.

He didn't seem overly slick. But he sized up everything like it was lying to him.

"Manager always break down boxes?"

"This one does."

"Is there somewhere quiet we can chat about the issue at hand?"

We couldn't talk on the dock. Union maintenance guys and the chefs paraded in and out of the dock doors. I took him to the storeroom. It was a massive space with metal shelves full of dry goods—spices, condiment packets, cups, straws, canned goods, etc. We stood by an industrial sized box of saltines and he asked me why I had suddenly accrued eleven thousand dollars in my bank account.

"Excuse me? How would you know anything about my bank account?"

"You throw a lot of informative paper away. Interested persons can pick up lots of paper just walking around behind apartment buildings, you know?"

I did throw the first deposit slip away. This Chessman guy dumpster-dived to weasel me out.

"Where did the eleven thou come from?" he asked. "Can you account for its origins? You know that there's a lot of money missing in this internal audit. You'll have to prove it wasn't skimmed. That's like Dumbass Embezzler Basics—don't deposit large sums of cash."

"Do I seem like a dumbass to you? If I stole anything, I wouldn't put it in a bank."

I was in a jam. I could say I got the money from a client (Mr. Dinosaur) through legal means (catering). But then he'd want work documents, menus, a copy of the check, he'd want to chat with Mr. Dinosaur. What was I suppose to do, call up Mr. Dinosaur and tell him to do me a solid? Absurd.

"Listen, for what it's worth," Chessman said, "I don't think you're a good suspect, other than this weird sum of money. But, hey, people are weird. They got other jobs, investments, whatever. My job isn't to blast hard working people. My job is to find the missing money for Starboard and implicate the thieves who stole it. You want to stay out of trouble? Help me."

This was starting to get heated for a storeroom conversation. I asked him to visit some other time, or somewhere else. I didn't feel comfortable talking about this fifty feet from my boss's office.

"Starboard doesn't care about making its employees uncomfortable if that means squeezing the truth from them." Well okay then. I wondered if that wouldn't make a better slogan for the company than the current one. *Starboard Catering: We'll take you with us.* Instead: *Starboard Catering: We'll squeeze the fucking truth out of you.* Chessman pulled a business card from his shirt pocket and wrote down his hotel info. He was in town for a few more days and was coming back the next day to look at the books and have a long "sit down" with Andy Rodnicki. (If Rodnicki sticks around, I thought. I could see him packing his kids and wife into a Ford Econoline and heading for the Far Frozen North.)

If he was trying to implicate me in the embezzlement and scare the sweet piss out of me—he did good work. Chessman made it clear that unless I complied (which meant telling about the eleven thou, which I did get fair and square… sort of) and helped prove Rodnicki's guilt, I was hosed.

When Chessman left, I was still in the far corner of that store room. It was a massive room, high ceilinged with caged pendulum lights way up there, and I always needed an angled safety ladder to reach the uppermost shelves. Mostly Styrofoam cups and straws went up there. That room was, for me, a good place to think. Sound was absorbed easily by all the cardboard, so it felt like you were compressed and contained.

And yet, now I knew I couldn't leave the job or town, even if I had the chutzpah to, because some in-house detective was nosing up my ass because of Rodnicki's wrongdoing. Excellent. Everything I'd gone through in the past two days—which was, I felt, a lifetime's worth of stress and nightmare for any sane individual—would perhaps be for nothing if the money was taken or frozen. I reached behind me and pulled out a single pack of saltines we served with Cobb salads. I tore it with my teeth and ate one. The raspy crunch of it filled my head. It was made louder in that surround of cardboard. That was why I didn't rightly hear what happened next.

It sounded like somebody was sliding a box, trying to heft it up and then dropped it a few aisles over. Problem was, the room was so clogged with inventory on the shelf, it was impossible to see in between them like you might do at a library. But there was someone in there with me. I'd been in that room too many times not to notice how the air changes or the poured concrete floor reverberated with footsteps. This was the sound of a box shifting off a shelf. I crouched to see underneath all the metal shelving along the floor. Nothing. Someone had stuffed more boxes underneath.

"Hey, someone else here? It's Cade."

Nothing again. The door to the storeroom was on the opposite angle of where I was and to leave I'd have to go to the far wall, and then all the way to the right.

There was the creaking of wood. Like leaning too hard on an old dining table. The joints of contact giving in and moaning. There was no wood in the storage room, though. I grabbed the largest thing next to me, a huge gallon of soy sauce, and started to make my way, slowly and quietly, up this aisle to the last row that led to the exit. A heavy clacking noise followed my steps. I stopped. It almost sounded like high heels, but no one who worked at Starboard wore heels to work. A thought entered my mind fully formed, a thought that made me drop the remaining cracker I'd forgotten about and clutch the bottle of soy sauce closer to my chest—

The wingback chair is in the storage room with me.
Mr. Dinosaur is.
That dark shape reflected in the spoon is.

Then, I thought: *But what the hell could it do to me—comfort me to death? How the hell did a chair get in here?*

That thought was immediately rebuffed by everything I knew about Mr. Dinosaur, which was: Be afraid. Be Very Afraid. The galloping sound from the Toothaker and from outside my apartment door earlier that morning came up from behind me a few aisles back. But this tramping had a wooden clog-like *klack* to it, and almost as if it couldn't keep its grip on the smooth floor.

I ran.

When I reached the corner, I slid to a stop and smashed my shoulder on a box of glass ketchup bottles. I could see in two directions all the way to the ends of the storage room. To the left was the exit. To the right was where I'd talked with Chessman. I peered down the first crosswise aisle—empty. I inched forward. When I looked toward the door, something along the far wall moved. It was a limb. An arm. I followed it up its length. There stood a shape over twelve-foot-tall standing behind the shelves covered in the same sheet as Mr. Dinosaur wore previously. Behind it was a reflective black surface like vertical oil and all poked throughout were winking suns glowing pink, blue, green, bleeding light and sucking it right back in. Every sun was a bleeding mouth and inside each mouth was a seething ball of knotted bodies and each pore in each body was a mouth that tried to tear and bite the one next to it. All was pain. From under the tented sheet, a long-fingered hand unraveled like a tongue and reached out and came down upon me—

"McCall!"

Rodnicki stood in the doorway in classic boss fashion. Hands on hips, chewing one end of his *Magnum, P.I.* mustache. "In my office, now." He poked his head further into the room. "And have a maintenance guy clean this shit." His office was stuffy. It smelled tart with sweat and smoke. There was a farty headnote as well. The office was cramped and suffocating. An ashtray by his keyboard overflowed with stubbed butts. He lit a fresh one as we spoke.

"Listen, looks like we're staring down the barrel of an internal audit. I don't know if you heard anything about this, but it could be bad for us. They got some inspector eyeballing our books. And, I think, looking pretty closely at you."

"At me? Why? I don't keep the books. Lorraine does."

Rodnicki pointed a finger at me and narrowed his eyes. As if he needn't say it. Lorraine wasn't in this. Not anymore.

"Funny that," he said. "Your job lists bookkeeping. And your signature is on the ledger." The smile he gave me was the kind that acknowledged guilt and took a nasty greasy joy in it.

"Should anything illegal be going on," I said, "I will not be a part of it. And I will not take the fall for it."

He didn't speak, he just smoked. He tapped the ash and told me that if I was going to take a truck or hot boxes for a personal gig, not to let other employees clean up my mess, which means he saw Keller cleaning up from the Toothaker. I told him I took some of the stuff home to clean it and fix it. I said I didn't use work items for personal gain.

Rodnicki got my meaning. He smiled. He relented.

"I'll admit, that's smart. That way we don't outsource

routine maintenance. But you still didn't tell me. Don't do it again."

This guy was a walking contradiction. He wouldn't push me on the embezzlement. He was too scared.

"Oh," he added, as I got up to leave, "Lorraine said you still haven't bought a new answering machine. We needed it yesterday. Who knows how many gigs we might be missing."

"I thought Lorraine didn't work here?"

Unable to counter with a proper answer, he said, "Get back to work, McCall."

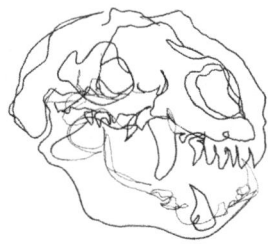

ELEVEN

I did not go back to work. I drove to the office supply store on the other side of town. And before that, I got drive-thru burgers and fries and ate in my car. I hadn't eaten anything in over twenty-four hours. Maybe more. I was so hungry that I drove through and got three more burgers and two fries. When I ate those, I licked the bag inside out of the remaining salt. I contemplated chewing on the paper bag when I caught myself. I wadded the bag and tossed it in the back. I had another uninvited vision of myself slurping down the bright smoke. But I knew it was inside me already.

I wept.

At the office supply store, I had to dodge the croaky-voiced college kid who kept asking me if I needed any help. I was a regular there, getting crap for the office: printer paper, timecards, pencils. I instinctively checked the far wall for signs of the Galactic Storeroom Man. He decided office supplies were boring, too, I guess, and skipped this place. I found the answering machines and was reading the back of the box, when I heard the crackle of static. Then the manager's voice came over the loudspeaker announcing a sale on pocket calculators. The static disappeared.

"There you are!" the sales associate said. He was winded from looking for me. "Anything I can help you with?"

"Not really. Found it."

The college kid frowned. Literally suffering with disappointment.

"I'll tell you about that model," he said.

"Please, don't. I already read the box. This'll do."

"Are you sure, that one's got so many bells and whistles now that—"

"Hey," I read his nametag, "Sean? Leave me alone."

Sean the Sales Associate scowled and moved past me to ask another victim how they wanted their shopping ruined by his presence.

Waiting in the checkout line, I heard the static of the speaker again. But no one was talking. Some idiot had elbowed the TALK button and was letting the white noise take over. The registers were unmanned, down to a single solitary one and the line was preposterously long for an office supply store at lunchtime. But everyone else was like my sorry ass, having to do their decrepit boss's duties during their own single, dwindling private hour. Every customer looked like they had gastrointestinal problems.

When I finally reached the front of the line, the curly-haired cashier gal was relieved by her manager, and yup, Sean the Master Associate took the keys. Before I was able to set the new answering machine down, the Manager—a frumpy, middle-aged masturbator with hair oil leaking into his polo collar—leaned into Sean's ear and (loud enough for me to glean) said that if he didn't straighten out the dot matrix printer display before closing, he'd lose his weekend hours and no lunch breaks.

My knuckles whitened. I felt my gut froth with nuclear rage. I wanted to chew this manager's nose off and spit it into the register drawer. The static in the overhead speaker crackled. Sean's face tightened then went loose with a well-worn practice. He was the punching bag for this manager. I got it. I knew what was up. (The static grew louder. I heard the voice say *Hello...I am a member of an, ah, extreme food...ah, specific catering services. I thank you. Ahhhhh*) I didn't like it. But I identified it. After Manager Cock left, I was still holding the machine to my chest (the static intolerably loud...*Mr. Dinosaur,* the voice announced), I got up in Sean's pimpled teenage face and told him, "Never let a motherfucker like that tell you what to do because there are some people with mouths who'll eat everything you own and never look back and the only way to put that shit down is nail them down hard the first time. You understand me? You gut those sonuvafucks." I made a slicing noise and motion upward. Sean nodded crazily and rang up my item. I tossed a fifty at him and told him to keep the change.

"You're a good kid. Quit this job ASAP."

I didn't want to open the box in the car. I knew what was waiting for me. I drove to work to drop it off. Most everyone was gone except for Keller and a few other chefs finishing for gigs later that night. I finally pulled the machine out and it was abuzz with busy noises. Not plugged in, naturally. The button alerting new messages blinked. I pressed it and Mr. Dinosaur's fluid and clotted voice emerged.

Cade McCall. It is nice to hear you listening. I require you this evening. Please find me waiting at the Golden Forest Cemetery.

No food. No dessert. Just me. I felt like I'd tried crack and couldn't quit smoking all day, every day. What was this compulsion I had? Why me?

Every pore in my body had a mouth. And in that mouth was a hunger for the next mouth's teeth. I would tear myself apart. This is how I felt.

I wanted to touch, to drink, to bathe in that vertical oil

that coated the far wall in the storeroom. I wondered what it felt like to wear a coating of it.

My only living hope was that at least Sean the Super Associate at Office Supply World would heed my advice, light that youthful fire in his tender underbelly, and flee for a place where the sky didn't bite and kept its jaws hidden. Until, that is, you were an adult and tall enough to have your head bitten off.

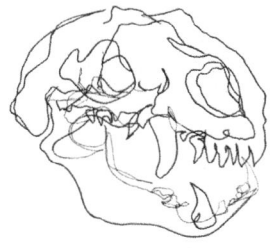

TWELVE

I had hours to kill. I called Tina to see if she wanted to get pie at Smitty's or just talk. But her phone rang endlessly. She refused to set up an answering machine. Probably for the best at this point. I drove to her apartment building but she wasn't home. So I wrote a handwritten message on the fast food bag from earlier. I scribbled some half-earnest plea for her love, but it ended up sounding goofy and playful. I quoted some lyrics from The Cure. The oily paper folded easily and I shoved it into her mailbox slot.

In her honor, I played *The Head on the Door* in my car.

I drove the next town over to the community college. They had a research library, and I wanted to look something up that had been scratching at the walls of my skull since Big Tiny Keller mentioned it. Those disappeared biker gangs. Something seemed off about that. Why would Keller even bring it up? I'd heard about a few gangs back when I was a kid. They'd sell drugs or act as bodyguards for bands that played massive house parties or the local colleges. There were always stories of hired assassinations, too. I remember kids like Billy Ballantyne in high school telling me at lunch that the gangs were into satanic sacrifice. It was inane, but I'm sure he felt a thrill passing on provocative gossip like that. Now I wasn't so sure it was gossip. I mean, I knew it wasn't.

The research librarian set me up with a microfiche machine and years of past issues of the local papers. I must've visited the soda machine three times and the coffee machine double that. It helped that college libraries were more like punk rock clubs and stayed open until 1 a.m. or later. And, so far as I could see, it was just me and the librarian behind her circular wooden desk in the next room.

The newspapers had reported on plenty of the crimes that the Motormouths and the Dragons got busted for. The Fuck Offs took up less space, if any. And it wasn't because of their colorful name. They seemed to evade all law enforcement.

There was a spate of animal brutalization in the

late 70s and early part of the 80s. Liquor store hold-ups. Rapes, shootings, and random assaults all attributed to the Motormouths and Dragons. Rival biker fights and shootouts at far out farmlands where county sheriffs were unlikely to intervene.

By early 1983, though, I could find nothing about any biker gangs. Except—for one very short piece. In it, the reporter merely commented on how the absence of the local gangs had been a blessing for many local businesses and the PTA. Casual drug use among teens had (seemingly) gone down (yeah, right). But there was nothing telling, no flaming arrow of a fact, waiting to be noticed and yanked out of the wall.

I wondered what it would be like to cater a biker gang get-together.

Would there be lots of casseroles and dips or would they just ask for slabs of raw meat and tubs of nitric acid? How does one even decide on table settings for a client called the Motormouths? Lots of cute little bike patches for the leather jackets or freshly decapitated heads on a platter of lettuce? Hard to say.

I was getting nowhere and my legs tingled, my ankles ached, and my bladder was a tense, tight fruit. Apparently, students of the college didn't frequent the library much, and the staff turned off every other row of lights to save money. Made me sleepy, even though it was earlier in the night.

When I stood up to stretch, I noticed a man in the room with me. He was standing in a corner over by a potted palm next to the Xerox machine. He had his back turned to me, but looked deep in some book. I went to the research librarian's desk and asked if I could use her phone for a moment. I lied and said I forgot change. "I really shouldn't," she said, but at the same time, without bothering to look, she put the phone up on the counter for me. She was engrossed in a novel with a lurid cover. I called Big Tiny Keller. He answered. I asked him why the Fuck Offs weren't in the news? (The librarian *did* look up then. I made a sorry face.)

"You gotta remember, man," Keller said, "While the Motormouths and Dragons were whooping it up around the Midwest, the Fuck Offs had deep plans. Nose to the grindstone and all that." I heard him suck on a cigarette, blow it out. "They were into telescopes and astrology and shit."

"So, what does that mean, they didn't terrorize people, deal drugs, and kick dogs? Instead, they read palms or braided each other's hair?"

"Nah, nothing like that. It means—shit, McCall. Bikers have a lifestyle, right? They dig open roads. Brotherhood. The bike as a way of life. Drugs and crime are ways to fund that. The Fuck Offs did the biker life to fund this other thing."

"The star stuff?"

"Sort of, yeah."

He was being aggressively vague, I could tell. He did this when I asked if a menu item was done, and it was late by a half hour. He was so big, though. You couldn't really argue with him. He was thinking now. I could hear the clunky machinery of his lug brain through the fuzzy phone lines.

"Like, take the thing with the graveyard," he said.

I tensed. My forehead broke out in a sharp sweat that happens when I sleep under too many blankets. I asked what about it.

"Well, that sounds like shit they used to talk about. I mean, I wasn't there, okay? This is second-hand news. But they were not nice guys, obviously. They were the darkest of the local gangs. It's in their name, right? But that was their philosophy all the way. *Fuck off and die.* Not just for other folks, but for themselves, too."

"Sounds like suicide is their friend, then."

(Another, less kind look from the librarian. Despite no one else around, she tapped her wrist to have me hang up. I put a finger up in begging mode for another minute.)

"Yes and no," Keller said. "All the astronomy and astrology crap they got up to was in pursuit of some higher power that they wanted to bring to earth. I remember a guy I ran with whose relative was in the Fuck Offs said that they wanted to 'uncouple life from the living'—I remember that was exactly what he said because it made no fucking sense to me then, and still doesn't. But whatever, this shit doesn't matter about the graveyard thing anyway because that nonsense was a gas leak."

I balked.

"You said it wasn't a gas leak."

"Hah. I changed my mind. A man's allowed."

"You changed it or it was changed for you."

"Does it matter? Hey, where are you anyway? Work?"

"What if I want more info on the star stuff they were doing? Who would I talk to?"

He was stumped. "Maybe this old biker named Tone-Bone. Let me dig up the number."

I said I'd swing by in the next hour. He said that was cool. And we hung up.

When I returned to my microfiche machine, that guy was still standing in the corner by the palm and copier. Same position. Still...reading? It had been at least fifteen minutes. I asked the librarian if the guy in the microforms room was a regular.

"What other guy?"

"The older guy in the room over here. He's been standing by the Xerox for a thousand years."

She said she had not seen anyone else other than me. Her face said that I needed to be an asshole somewhere else.

I told her I worried that maybe this guy was a perv, jacking off in public and whatnot. But, then, as I said it, he had been still as a mannequin. The librarian wasn't moved by my social concerns. She didn't think he was in there, and that I was messing with her. In order for myself not to be the pervy-weirdo, I then went back to my machine to get some of the change I lied about not having.

I needed more coffee.

Now this time the guy wasn't by the palm. He was nowhere.

Gone.

I was trying to sort out this new info about the biker gangs. Juggling the change in my hand. The snack machines were in the library's main lobby, past the front desk and through a set of double doors. There was a long hallway to my left for library staff offices, and to the right was a computer lab that was closed. The lights were off. The room hummed. All I could see were the green and red and blue lights of surge protectors and a few rows of brand new Compaqs. Their mice connected to them on their serving pads, waiting with tense patience to do their boss's bidding. In front of me was the row of doors that led outside, and in the night sky I could tell it was going to rain sooner than later. Trees swayed to the east. Trash and litter followed the wind through the quadrangle. A plastic shopping bag was hooked in the branches of an oak. It caught and blew open like a windsock.

I decided that plastic bag flying like a flag in the tree was the symbol for my new life. Plastic bags were made of oil. Oil was compressed dinosaur bones and plant life. The vertical wall of black oil. Hmm. Staring at all this quiet stuff got me thinking about why a biker gang would want a telescope. It made no sense to me. Good for them on continuing their education?

I put my thirty-five cents into the drink machine and pressed *Coffee with sugar*. The cup dropped. The machine spluttered. Hot water and coffee mix shot out. I scanned the floor for dropped coins. Habit. There was a quarter hiding right under the machine, totally in shadow. I felt like I won the lottery. I bent down to pick it up and spotted a piece of dirty cloth by it. I got further down to look under the machine. There was a pair of feet. They were crusted with dirt. Someone stood between the coffee and snack machines, which was nuts because there was only a half foot clearance between them. I left the quarter. My coffee was done, but I didn't touch it. I didn't want it anymore. I couldn't move. But then I thought: *if I never move, nothing bad can happen.* Ever. But I had to do it. I had to lean to the right and see what was wedged in between the machines.

I leaned so slowly, I heard my knees bend.

It was the man who'd stood by the copier. He was shoved so tightly in between the machines that it seemed impossible, like something from an Indiana Jones film. His head was down. His arms scrunched to his sides. He looked older, skinny. Depleted.

Then he started to wiggle. Like he was having a grand mal seizure. He was a piece of thin meat sizzling in hot fat. His head rose and his jaundiced eyes were wide and open. Copier Guy shimmied harder. The machines that sandwiched him in rocked on their rubber-booted feet. I fell back and called for the librarian, but those double doors to the inner library blocked most noise. On purpose. It was a library, after all. Copier Guy had worked a leg out. Shaking. When I saw the shoeless and grimy foot, I knew this guy was dead. He was moving like his body had been hooked up to a car battery. He jittered and shook. As he did, his eyes were locked on me. And they were pleading. His expression was one of need, of desperation. He wanted help.

I was (do I need to say it?) too terrified to move. Fight or flight or freeze. I wanted him to quit shaking. If he didn't move, I could think.

But he shivered and shook as if he was hypothermic, left out on an open wintry plain. My inner mammal gave up and headed for the doors going out. I slammed into the fire bar and waited in that in-between space with the shoe mats and announcement boards. I don't know why I wasn't gone already. I wanted to see if Copier Guy would follow. Or begin running. Finally, the two machines like a pair of thighs shat him out, gyrating, onto the floor. He held a coat, a blazer, one I assumed he was buried in. He was painfully thin and sable-haired. Now, he looked nothing like my parents or any relative I've ever had. But he obviously was, at some point, a human related to other humans. Why I developed such an empathetic heart in this moment is entirely confounding—but, I think it was all of my thinking about Mr. Dinosaur. He was, so far as I could tell, here among us to destroy order. To do what he wanted to do was unfathomable. Literally. I had no brain space for it. Somehow, I knew that this fella, this man, wasn't a Compaq, he was the mouse tied to it unwillingly.

I set myself one rule: the minute this fucker tried to bite or claw or maim me—I'd be out the doors to Splitsville.

He watched me like a dog, a hungry dog.

Ehh.

But still, he wasn't nipping. I opened the door and walked a few feet toward him. He turned and almost lost his balance.

"What's your name?"

As slow as you please, like a delicate geezer in an old folks' home, he placed a finger to his lips. He tried pushing it in. Wouldn't go. I stepped a little closer. He grew more animated, wanting help. He dropped the blazer. Both hands were at his mouth. But he shook too much. I thought about how no movie or book or comic book I ever read or watched had prepared me for a moment like this. I had zero training or intuition. Still, I reached my hand out to take his. To steady it.

It was—and forever has been—the coldest thing I'd ever held in my life. It was hard not to let go. And nothing I did would put heat into this man's hands. The skin was equal parts sallow and bluish and pale. He felt like stiffened clay. He smelled of closed-up basements and dry leaves. A mouthful of unbrushed teeth. This was hard going. I wanted to cry from discomfort. The man seemed equally disturbed. But he'd stopped shaking.

"Is that better?"

The man nodded, slightly. The skin of his face had shrunk in an aggressive way. Pulling his nose up a bit, giving his eyes a fierce stare. The mouth cast downward. I picked up his jacket but there was no wallet or anything in it, of course. Everything crumbled with dirt and loose pebbles. Then he took my hand, slow, and brought it to his mouth. I jerked it away and backed up. The man's hands went to his sides, his head, dejected. As if I'd misunderstood his intentions. I caught his eye.

"Don't fucking bite me, pal. Okay?"

Again, he reached and took my index finger now. He brought it to the crease between his lips, which were dry pathetic things, like grazing one's finger against the surface of any inanimate smooth surface. But I felt a pluck of string. And then I knew what he wanted. Mortuary services had sewn his lips shut for his funeral. Once I got it, I dug my finger around and popped a loose stitch. A corner of his mouth loosed open. The rest were harder to work out, so I ran to the librarian's desk and asked for a pair of scissors.

"Are you going to finish soon? If no one's here by 11:30 p.m., they let me close early."

"Yeah, yeah, one sec."

With the scissors, it was easy to snip his mouth open. He worked his mouth and jaw, for the first time in, who knows how long? I asked his name again. Nothing. I jogged around him, remembering my coffee, and gestured for him to take it. I didn't know if dead people could drink. Or, if they did, what would happen to them. I'd heard that pigeons exploded if you gave them rice. Maybe it was the same with corpses and coffee.

Copier Guy gave the steaming coffee a longing look, took it, and stiffly poured some into his body. It was not drinking. That required a kind of humanly grace. This was brute throwing back of liquid into a hole. I took the cup from him. He didn't seem to hate or love the coffee either way. He gave a glassy stare. I wanted to return the scissors but Copier Guy stepped after. I stopped.

"No, no, no. Stay here."

I moved.

Copier Guy moved.

"Buddy. No go. Stay put."

When I handed over the scissors to the librarian, she said, "Tell that guy if he wants to stay here, he has to wear shoes. It's a state law."

I laughed at this. She was not pleased.

"Yeah, sure. I'll tell him. State law. Right."

I ushered Copier Guy to my Toyota, but I was still unsure about him. I popped the trunk and gently pushed him in and laid a roadside blanket over him. He gazed at me like an injured deer. He wouldn't know the difference. Not much different than where he'd been spending his time all those years before, I guessed. Also, if I got pulled over, I wasn't interested in explaining why my uncle here smelled like rotten ass and was leaking coffee from the holes where the mortician pumped him full of embalming fluid.

As I started the car, I realized that I didn't care if I lost my job or if Rodnicki tanked the business. What did any of that matter compared to what I'd experienced in the past two days? Or what I was sure to learn in the coming day or two? I marveled at how we, everyone, pretended to be King Shit in our everyday lives when really we were just galactic varnish on some more monstrous and vast body, simply an electric jelly sneezed into space demanding all protons and electrons come to their knees for our whims. It was a dark feeling, and an even worse admission. I wanted to spurn myself for it. Yet I couldn't. I owned it. I felt an older, more normal part of Cade McCall die away. I wondered if that was due to my connection with Mr. Dinosaur, Copier Guy, or years working with my dickhole boss. Either way, it was done, and I had to deal with it.

    I didn't have time to stop by Keller's.

    I had a date at the graveyard.

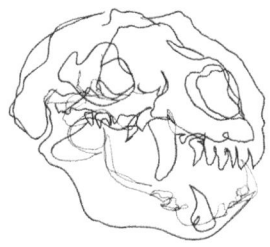

THIRTEEN

The Yellow Suit Brigade had already packed up their toys and gone home. Golden Forest Cemetery was not under immediate state investigation anymore. Or federal, I guessed. There was a lone cop at the main gate. Visiting hours were over way before I pulled up. There was no other way in, that is, unless I wanted to scale the outer wall. I'd either leave Copier Guy in the trunk or throw him over. Neither prospect seemed all that grand to me. I decided to try my luck with the cop. I rolled down the window and he gave me a spiel about hours and the explosion and—

"You Ballantyne's friend?" he said.

"What? Yeah, I was visiting him earlier."

The cop glanced back at the graveyard as if he was keeping an eye on it.

"What you need to do in there?"

"Sounds weird, but I like to jog at night. Peaceful, you know?"

"In those clothes?"

I threw my head back to the trunk, indicating sweats. He nodded, then waved me through.

"Just steer clear of the taped off area."

I had no idea where I was to meet Mr. Dinosaur. I drove without my lights on not to draw too much suspicion from the cop. I drove by the taped area anyway. The inspectors had left their giant lights and some official junk around. Trash bags stuffed with who knows what. Fast food litter. Much of it had blown into the massive hole.

Mr. Dinosaur did that, I thought. Somehow, he did that.

Irritated, I kept winding around the narrow driving paths, going further back into the graveyard into the thicker area of older mausoleums and the hillier part of the land. Deer scattered across the road. Groundhogs and wild turkeys flushed out and scurried back into hiding spots. But it was from the corner of my eye that I noticed a pyramidal mausoleum with an open door. That cursed wingback stitched with acanthus leaves and lotus blossoms was leaning against the smooth stone. The torn up and knifed back of it was up a small, steep hill among older crooked gravestones and plots. So old that the shifting earth had them buckling sideways. Here and there, some plots had battery-powered candle lights twinkling their vigils.

I did not feel comforted. Neither did the dead.

I approached the pyramid, which had to be nearly twenty feet tall, easy. The door was massive and steel. I heard rasping from inside, a rollicking and wet clapping inside. Laying half in and half out of the door's gap was a dead raccoon. It opened its mouth and words came out.

"Welcome. Thank you for, ah, coming," the raccoon head/Mr. Dinosaur said. I found it hard to be shocked at this point. The raccoon's mouth barely moved. Its words rattled and fell out of the dead animal as foul gas from a corpse.

"Did you do that?" I pointed back toward the explosion site. "Was that your doing?"

"Yes. I ate it just as I will eat another part. Then another and another."

"Why?"

"That is who I am. That is what I do. This...form I must inhabit to sink among you is...unworthy. Constricting."

"What's your true form?"

"You do not have the right eyes for that. Or brain. And 'form' is the wrong word, entirely. But do not worry,

Mr. McCall. You have been supremely helpful. I always need help. For when I eat, I become slow. I am depleted. I have told you this. That is why I always reach out to those who are, ah, in need. You are bound." The raccoon's dead tongue was dragged across, or licked, its lips. It didn't blink. I remember that it never blinked.

"Bound how? I don't owe you anything."

"Yes, you do. You owe me everything." It gestured meekly to indicate the graveyard. Though I wondered if it meant all humanity. My brain boiled from the closeness to Mr. Dinosaur. The wings of the chair leaning on the pyramid flexed and moved. And the feet of it nestled around in the dirt, as if reveling in the cold feeling.

"Will you leave?" I asked.

"When I am finished eating."

"The dead."

"Everything. I start with the dead, as you have seen. But I will end with the hot core of this world, then the sun, then the space where all of those have been. In fact, that is why I have asked you here. You have much to do, Cade McCall. But together we will finish this great and grand job."

Instantaneously, as if it'd cracked open my skull and shoved reams of files into it, I saw names upon names, with faces associated with them. It was the dead, the mighty dead spread out like a corpse-sewn blanket beneath our feet.

It turned its heavy, heavy head—for I knew its head

was as heavy as a moon, even if it pretended to be a raccoon. "Stop worrying. This is not the first place I have taken, nor will it be the last."

I wanted to wail. I felt my will clot inside whatever I considered my soul. I assumed whatever soul I had was pinched between Mr. Dinosaur's fingers.

"Are the things that follow me yours?"

"The chair was a requirement to make sure you understood me. Simple, but effective. Whatever else has followed you is not of my watch."

"The dead," I said. "The dead follow me."

"That could be. They know you now. And sometimes the dead slip out of my mouth. Remnants have been known to last and escape, yes. Do you have one? Bring them to me. I will take care of it." The wingback writhed next to the mausoleum.

When it said that, Mr. Dinosaur's raccoon flickered for a moment, the way a VCR jittered and the tracking went wonky. For a blink, it vanished, the whole thing, and I could sense an immensity so deep and wide and thoroughgoing that I wanted to cut my own head off not to feel it. The vastness was at the core of the earth and I knew, if I looked hard enough, Mr. Dinosaur's form stretched and would also be thwacking and thwipping through the sky. I had a sudden image of a long tail or nerve or tongue waving along the length of space between earth and the moon. I snapped into focus.

Mr. Dinosaur's raccoon was still sitting, massive yet brittle, in the chair. I walked to the Toyota and brought out Copier Guy. I lead him around the gravestones up the hill. His cadaver-cold hand trembled in mine. But not from lack of a blanket. He resisted. I had to tug him along. His mouth geared along, opening and closing, the little ragged ends of the mortician's thread flapping off his lips. I couldn't know what he meant to say or thought. But as we neared closer, he fell back into the shakes. Those horrible tremors that helped work his way from between the machines at the library. It was fear. The dead man was afraid in a new way by the proximity to Mr. Dinosaur—and yet I still brought him closer, though a voice deep in my conscience said,

You're killing him all over again! STOP!

Now Copier Guy was as uncontrollable as one of the last popcorn kernels in a Jiffy Pop bag. Spinning and spasming. Unable to blossom. Mr. Dinosaur thought it was all in good fun. A light, rabid, dead raccoon smile. And quick as a frog's tongue, it reached out its small free claw that extended with a mutated *thwick* and brought the dead man into the dark.

I was happy not to be obliged to feed it again. What follows was heard, not seen. I imagined that Copier Guy's arm was already in Mr. Dinosaur's jaws and clamping shut. The snap I heard reminded me of when I used to camp with my family, and I had to gather the sticks for a fire. My father would take the biggest ones, lay them diagonally on the picnic table, then jump on them to halve them. *SNAP!* It was a dry and sharp sound. There would be no blood. Copier Guy would be in a frenzied flail. His hand would fall to the ground uneaten, unloved, in a way. Mr. Dinosaur now had the corpse gripped at its mid-section and his finger sank into the body as if it was a child's plush animal—and his mouth tore open to show that black gape, that unreflective hole, and it clamped down over the corpse's left shoulder and part of its head. There would be no chewing. Just biting and some form of swallowing. His teeth were tiny points of antilight. And each of those points had their own vast ridges of energetic teeth which spanned for miles.

I knew then that any emotional sadness I felt was merely the slow evolution of chemicals and acids and particles weaving and dancing so blindly through time and meeting so purely by chance in that dance, that to deny the meaningless providence of it, the sheer opacity of hurt it was meant to calculate, was to deny the process altogether. One thousand million years had unfolded themselves to this moment of pain and decision.

The levels of death that the action entailed had me on my knees. I was crying so hard I could not see the ground before me. But I heard the crackle of Mr. Dinosaur's voice, as if it was on an answering machine. The sound popped and sizzled in my headvoice. *Mr. McCall, it is best you go now, before I finish, and continue with your work*—my work, which I knew,

knew, meant collecting what was left behind by the dead and bringing it to Mr. Dinosaur to eat. I imagined a child slurping up a long strand of pasta. That was a life. And the tip in the mouth was merely the corpse. The rest of the strand was the long, wriggling chain of objects and ephemera that we accrued around us the whole way. I was weak with such an impossible and infinitesimal task.

I had enough gall to spit out that I couldn't do it. I didn't want to do it.

"I won't do this for you," I said.

The bright smoke emerged from the pyramid and filled the hill.

In my head Mr. Dinosaur spoke: *I eat so slowly that the end of everything on this planet is a distant memory of the future but there is nothing to stop me from keeping you alive until it is over. Your suffering will add up to more than what has been propagated through human existence. Do this or account for your insubordination.*

For all that I came to know before Mr. Dinosaur, I knew I was not powerless. My abilities were a speck on the windshield of a god. But they were still alive.

The raccoon head slid wetly and silently back into the pyramid and the door slammed.

I was to know something then, something given by Mr. Dinosaur. I was to know that I was the only one to respond to the call it gave. Intuitively, I knew that millions of people all over the globe received a similar broken, crackling message, but me, I, idiot Cade McCall, answered back.

I brought this on myself. From the beginning.

I stumbled to my car and drove the paths to the gate, where the cop waved me on into the night. I kept thinking *to uncouple life from the living to uncouple life from the living to*
uncouple
life
from
the
living

I was a way down the road when the explosion erupted behind me in the graveyard.

Mr. Dinosaur had taken a second bite.

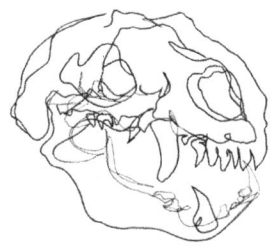

FOURTEEN

I heard emergency services barreling toward the Golden Forest. Ambulances, police cars, fire trucks. Mr. Dinosaur wouldn't be there, of course. Who knew where it—he?—them?—would be. A massive crater pocking the face of the town was where Mr. Dinosaur had last sat.

Big Tiny Keller opened the door of his place before I knocked on it. Seeing another human, so soon after the library and graveyard, buoyed me like I hadn't expected. All this shit that'd happened to me—the weight of it was soaking every brain cell and squashing every rational sentence I could utter. Keller must've heard me pull up. He already had his boots, coat, and keys. "We're taking my truck," he said. It was a massive red and white Ford F-150 with jacked-up wheels. He was a big guy, as his name implied, and the truck was the only machine that housed him perfectly. Taking his truck meant two things: where we were going was a risk to him, so he could leave if he wanted, and he wanted to listen to his music, which invariably those past few years in rural Indiana was John Cougar Mellencamp. Thumping drums and dark chiming guitar didn't help my mood, but it was a welcome distraction. We'd get to "Small Town" shortly anyway.

"You look like shit, McCall." He looked over. "No offense."

"None taken."

"Tone-Bone's home. But we can't spend too much time there."

"Alright."

I realized I was staring at Keller. I wanted to tell him everything that had happened to me. But what could I do? What would he say? Likely he'd laugh, smoke, and ask me to elaborate on how the corpse was eaten. Though I could see something deep inside him that compelled him to believe. The way he talked about the gas leak. Hell, even his driving me out to the middle of the sticks to see this biker. Or biker's widow, or whatever.

Even sitting in the cab of the Ford, I felt Mr. Dinosaur's pull somewhere above me. It was spread over the whole land like acid rain or a cancerous cloudbank. But he was also underneath in the water pipes and sewage drains and curled up among the root systems of trees and mushrooms. Air, land, and sea. All of it compromised, all of it captured.

"That inspector, Chessman, called me again. Wanted to know about your relationship with Rodnicki."

Oh, Christ on a cracker. I forgot about this nonsense.

"What did you tell him?"

"That you two are like warring countries, man. He asked if I thought it was put on, like you two were faking it to steal money. I told him to get fucked."

"No, you didn't."

Pause.

"No, I didn't. But that was the gist of what I said."

"I have a feeling that guy won't back off. He has it in for me. I don't know why. He thinks I'm stealing money. Why would I do that?" Indeed—why would I ever do anything again after today? I was willing myself to say the words I said through my mouth. Which is crazy. But every globule of cellular stuff inside me wanted to be elsewhere in service of Mr. Dinosaur.

"I don't know. Why would you? Shit, McCall. Rodnicki does it because he and his wife want to be big fish in a small pond. You? You're pondless. You couldn't give a shit about ponds."

This was something I thought of a lot—and though I never gave it credence or approved of it, I understood it. Living in small town America, especially in the Midwest, was a sort of two-sided badge. On one side, people were proud of it. It somehow conferred honesty and a warm heart on you, whether or not you had either. Outside of the Midwest, people were more liable to treat you as a folksy farmer than as a person with ambitions beyond agriculture, country music, and church. The flip side was that you felt less-than, were treated as such, and had no way to prove this than to become what your accusers were—non-Midwesterners. Or—you could dismiss all of this and see it as so much psycho-social-political mumbo jumbo. But for some people—like the Rodnickis—that self-esteem complex ramped up and made them do things against their better judgment, knowing that they'd never fit in outside the small town—they worked, scraped, scammed their way into the biggest possible slot inside the small town. Happened all the time. And now the consequence of it was probably going to get either Andy and me fired or bring down the business.

Then again: it was hard for me to really care anymore.

No one would've cared much about money or business, if they knew they were all slowly dying and were the pawns of a...I don't even know what Mr. Dinosaur was. A god, a devil, an alien, a solar system come to life? Who the hell knew.

Its teeth. Its mouth. However large. However expansive. Just pressing down lightly. Teething on the skin of the earth. The gullet long. Dark. Forever.
    We drove with the music going until the tape stopped, flipped, and resumed. By the time "R.O.C.K. in the U.S.A." kicked on and blew off, we were heading down a skinny rural route with deep drainage ditches on either side of the road. The air smelled like turned dirt, cinnamon, and wisps of wood smoke. I had no idea where we were. I said so.
    "Good. Tone-Bone's not interested in having people drop by anytime they like."
    "Paranoid?"
    "You could say that. But for good reason."
    "Why?"
    "I'll let Tone explain."
    The surface road lead onto an unmarked gravel road that I'd have missed if I was by myself. This wound around in a thick wood, breaking out into a field every so often. Then Keller said he missed a turn.
    "Where?"
    He threw the truck in reverse and put his arm up on the bench seat to look over his shoulder.
    "There."
    It was a two-track dirt path, not a road, with a mohawk of grass and growth blocking it. There was no way the person who lived back here left their home or that anyone came to

see them. I'm surprised Keller remembered where all the turns were. Another few minutes on this path and he nodded in satisfaction. "Here we go." He turned off the truck and we got out. We faced nothing. It was a stand of trees. Crickets, a clutch of bullfrogs, total darkness. Way off in the distance, maybe I saw the moon, or the light from the top of a coal chute far away. "We walk to the house."

We hiked through a hundred yards of trees, saplings, milkweed, thistle, jimson weed, and whatever else till he stepped out onto a fairly well-mown yard. Not big, but decent. There was a house, a log cabin really, settled in the middle of it. Abandoned cars lined the edge. A few dogs barked at us as we approached, but despite their size and sound, they drove straight to Keller and licked his hands and he knelt to rub their snouts and ears. They were cautious around me but after they got my scent, we were pals. An older woman stood on the porch with a shotgun laid over her arm.

"Who's that?" I asked.

Keller scoffed. "That's Tone-Bone."

Tone-Bone was not fucking around. She was in her sixties but had the attitude of a twenty-year-old in a punk club. Her graying hair was swirled up into a knot on her head. She wore glasses. A torn Ramones shirt, cardigan, and hunting jacket over that. Something like clamdiggers and big wool socks inside of mud boots. Her arms were patched with tattoos and she had lots of earrings. There were no real lights outside the house other than her porch light, so she was waiting for us to get closer. She smiled at Keller when she recognized him. A front tooth was chipped.

"Tiny. Thought it was you." They hugged. I waited down the steps. "This the guy?"

He said it was.

"Come on in. Let's get a drink."

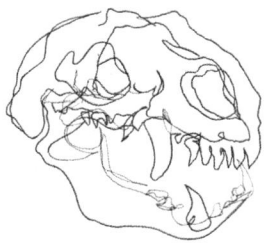

FIFTEEN

Here's what Tone-Bone told me over some jars of homemade moonshine.

The Fuck Offs were a biker gang comprised of women only. Really, the first one like it. And it was not one of these Sunday riders, donate to shelters, help all women and children, rah rah rah. No. This was a serious gang. The women were hardened. Half had done time in jail or federal women's pens. Most were career criminals. Many had never been caught. They carried guns, knives, and explosives everywhere they went. One thing that brought them all together, Tone-Bone said, was a hatred of anyone outside the gang. Sometimes even inside the gang, but that was different. They did and sold drugs. But since male gangs had sewn up the protection and bodyguard racket, they worked a different angle. They started hosting secret punk shows. Those shows made a little bit of money. So did drugs. The punk shows introduced them to occult freaks. Those freaks introduced the Fuck Offs to weirdo spiritualists and doomsayers and Satanism.

I said that what I had experienced wasn't Satanism.

"Shut up," Tone-Bone said. "I'm not done."

I didn't talk again until she asked me to speak.

Tone-Bone said that at the time the world was going downhill. The gang wanted to reflect that. They increasingly were anarchic and anti-natalist. But not only did they want people to stop making life, they wanted life to quit on the earth full stop. Not even the Satanists were for that. Satanists were good time folks.

But the gang knew someone. A self-described dark priestess who lived in a trailer on the Ohio River. The Fuck Offs found her—well, kidnapped her from Paducah, Kentucky. Brought her back to Indiana and forced her to show them how to find a way to stop life on earth without killing people themselves. They weren't murderous. They were genocidal. There was a difference. The Fuck Offs wanted the process of life halted. Reversed, maybe. Tone-

Bone didn't remember the priestess's name, but the priestess got them into astronomy. Their headquarters was like an amateur science club. Star charts, telescopes, radios. She had them building some kind of a henge, too, made out of old trashed cars welded together and whatnot. Tone-Bone was there for all of it and thought it was garbage. But fun. She hated people, obviously. Look at where she lived now. But the whole *let's reach out to the stars* thing had little sway on her. Still, she did it. Took part. Played the role.

Then the priestess started smoking a combo of opium and cleaning supplies. She started receiving visions of a being that lived in a star. She told the gang that this being, or beings like it, were what the Fuck Offs wanted. A reversal to existence.

"A ball of limbs with mouths in every pore," I said. I didn't mean to.

Tone-Bone turned. "That's exactly right, smart guy. You better wish you didn't know that."

She continued.

The Fuck Offs wanted a way to uncouple life from the living. The gang jumped on this and encouraged the opium-cleaning cocktail for weeks. At this point, Tone-Bone thought they'd lost sight of the goal. They were worshipping the priestess or themselves or this made-up star-god instead of trying to avoid systems and hierarchies altogether. So one day Tone-Bone split. Not much longer after that, the Fuck

Offs found the priestess in a coma; they dragged her body out to the broken carhenge and cut her chest open with a machete. They strew her guts around in a circle and hung her body up on a rusted Datsun. Tone-Bone said some bikers probably ate part of the priestess or drank her blood. More likely than not.

I waited for her to say something. Thinking she was done, Keller asked, "How do you know that happened?"

Tone-Bone stood up and went to a drawer in an old armoire. She pulled out a tape. She threw it at me. I caught it and read the label, written in someone's caveman scrawl.

It said: *the beginning*

"On that tape, which I've watched precisely *two* times, and you'll not get me to watch it anymore, you'll find the whole process I just described filmed and then transferred to videotape. The tape covers a week."

"A week? Why?"

"Because that's how long she kept breathing after they split her open."

Tone-Bone explained that whatever this thing was that was eating everything around them—this nothing made manifest—it had kept the priestess alive as a display of power.

But when this thing didn't show up, when nothing happened, they burnt the henge down and tried to move on to another money-making scheme. When the Motormouths and the Dragons heard about this, they teamed up to break apart the Fuck Offs. Scatter them forever. But it didn't work. Because the Fuck Offs were nowhere to be found. The other two gangs rolled up on the hideout and it was like Berlin 1945. Up and gone, man. Teamed up together to take out a gang that wasn't around, they then turned on each other. The shootout cut both gangs down to half.

When Tone-Bone got word of this, she burned all her Fuck Offs ID: her jacket, patches, she sold the bike to someone else. Didn't even ride a bike anymore. Just stayed on her little acre and grew food, dug a well, fed chickens, kept a still, etc.

"So that's it. That's what I got."

"Do you know what's been going on?"

"If it's past that tree line, I don't give a shit."

"Two explosions at the graveyard in town," Keller said. The first he'd expressed any concern about it.

Tone shrugged.

"Something's here," I said. "It eats the dead. But not just the dead. It eats their whole path through life. Does that make sense? It'll eat the rest of us next. I've fed it."

Her eyes perked up. "You're the next priestess, then, huh?"

I felt a tugging at my belly, a horrible sensation of being cut open alive by a biker gang and strung along the telephone wires like so much carrion. Like a prep table full of beef knuckles or turkey necks.

"No. I'm saying that I've been drawn into this thing. And I don't know how to get out or how to stop it."

"Whatever it was that those women summoned or called up or intercepted—it's not going away. It might take a break or slow down, but it ain't quitting on you."

"How do you know that?"

She pointed to her stomach. "This says so. Listen— I've got no answers, only suspicions. Who had the answers? The Fuck Offs did. And they're toast. Maybe one of the Motormouths or the Dragons has a story to tell—but good luck locating one of them, you know? And their old ladies aren't going to say word one to either of you. Maybe to me, but I ain't leaving here anytime soon. World's a mess out there."

In the other room, her dogs went wild with barking. Tone-Bone pulled a handgun from her waistband. She held it up and in front like a SWAT agent, moving step by step into a space off her living room. When she popped her head around, her danger fell away, but her face was in shock. Keller and I joined her. There was a movie playing on a bare wall, but we couldn't see where it was coming from. It should've come from a projector ten feet away, but there was no projector in the room.

"That's it," she said. "That's the goddamn video in your hand."

From what she described, the video matched. It was a

shaky recording taken at dusk. A woman was strapped to an upended truck and she looked disemboweled.

I had to turn my head away. One of her dogs nuzzled my knee.

"I should've never let you two come out here," Tone-Bone said. Her face gaunt. Her eyes yellowed in booze. Keller was watching, but painfully. He began trying to find where the image was coming from.

When I looked back up, I could tell—yes—the priestess was still breathing. Her eyes were open, and her mouth was slack. The camerawoman asked a question, but it was muffled. The priestess (though I was starting to wonder what that word even meant here) coughed clots of blood, green brown orange. A few women behind the camera made cheerful noises. The video from nowhere vanished.

We stood in the dark.

A phone rang. We all moved back into the living room. Tone-Bone went to the phone on the wall and picked it up. The ringing continued. "This isn't the phone that's ringing," she said, confused.

"Give me a break," Keller said.

Tone-Bone went to the armoire and opened the cabinets. Shifting magazines. Boxes. Baggies of weed. At the bottom under shoeboxes was an old rotary phone. *That* was ringing. It wasn't hooked up. She set it gently on the floor. I could hear the bells in it.

Tone-Bone was scared. When we pulled up, I thought she'd be the toughest human I'd ever meet. And now I saw she was as vulnerable as anyone else.

"What do we do?" Keller said.

"It's not going to stop," she said.

I didn't want to, but I said, "I'll answer it."

I really wanted this to be an atmospheric fluke, some sort of pinpointed seismic oddity. But I knew it wouldn't be. The dread in my body made it hard to move. I picked up the receiver from the cradle and put it to my ear. I heard the crackling first. A distant breaking of electrons. The convulsive breathing of a maniac on the edge of the solar system. I wondered where this was coming from, whose mouth, how far away, with what tongue? There was no voice, no message. That crush of electricity. I remembered that image I had of a tail wagging somewhere in the space between earth and the moon. I hung up the phone.

The three of us stood there staring at it. I still had the video in my hand. It felt heavy. I set it in the chair.

"Take that tape with you. And the phone. I don't want either of them in my house anymore. You want some unsolicited advice? Leave this thing alone. Run away. Hide. Find a boring hobby and bury yourself in it."

"Run where?"

She thought. She had no answer.

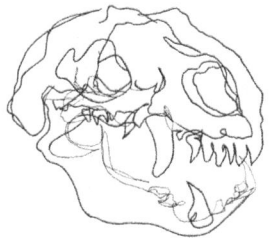

SIXTEEN

Against our better judgment, Big Tiny Keller and I showed up to work the next day. Everyone felt the tension of the internal investigator, Chessman, and his presence. He and Rodnicki (who was sweating magnificently) were talking and walking around a lot. Rodnicki refused to make eye contact with me. Which was fine. I'd had about enough human contact for a long time. I desperately wanted normalcy. I threw myself into arranging menus and working with venues for graduations, weddings, retirements. At no point was I lost in my work, or did I forget about what had happened, but the weight of what I knew was a tad lighter. When a client haggled with me about the price of scalloped potatoes for a first communion lunch, I smiled a little. That was a revelation. The smile fell when I remembered the twenty-two thousand in my bank account.

I should've been content. But it all seemed tainted.

Staring at the new answering machine, which was already accruing a light sheen of grease on it, and the signed photo from a second-rate Hollywood star, I thought of staring into Keller's burn barrel in his yard. When we returned from the country and to my Toyota, Keller had tossed the tape and phone into this barrel behind his house with scrub brush and leaves he'd collected over the weeks. The tape made a good crackle. The phone took longer.

Now my office phone rang. I pushed the chair back. I stared at the phone. *Did the cord to the headset wiggle?* No one was in the office with me. I caught a chef's eye through the big windows that looked out into the kitchen. The chef waited to see if I wanted anything. The phone seemed to ring harder. I waved this chef over. When they opened the office door and stuck their head in ("What's up?"), I picked the phone from the cradle and listened. Was this the way it was going to be? Afraid of ringing phones?

"Cade, you got a minute?" Rodnicki said.

"I do."

"Chessman would like to speak with you."

I hung up the phone. Dismissed the curious chef.

I was ready for that to be the last call I ever took at Starboard Catering. My desk would be easy to clean. That's how efficient and orderly I was. I would *not* miss being in the storeroom.

Kurt Chessman sat in a guest chair to the side of Rodnicki's desk. I sat in one of the two directly in front. That made a difference. People who were going to get punishment rained down on them never sat in the side seat. Chessman was calling some shots. I could see the disdain and bile in Rodnicki's face. He was chewing gum, loudly. He did this to remove the taste of menthol cigarettes he endlessly smoked. But also to dilute stress. His sweating had only doubled in its performance. If we were alone, I'd have recommended he not leave the office without throwing on his blazer.

"Thanks for meeting with us, Cade. This shouldn't take long," Chessman said. He was flipping back and forth between the pages of a yellow legal pad and his leather Franklin Planner. Rodnicki had his open, too. Dueling management planners. He sat across from me, leaning back, drilling a stare somewhere between the second and third button of my dress shirt. There was some brief introductory chatter about how well the unit was running. How pleased clients were. Chessman brought up the second explosion that rocked his hotel room. Crazy times in the Midwest, he said. Hopefully they get the gas lines under control. He transitioned seamlessly.

"I'm not sure how much you've been privy to..." Chessman said.

Surely, this was a performance for Rodnicki, at this point.

"...but I've discovered some irregularities in the finances of this unit of Starboard. Numbers passed up to the district office weren't matching what we projected, so, you know, they send me down for an official audit. No biggie. But it does turn out that these irregularities are much larger, more egregious, than previously expected."

My ass was sweating into the seat. *Just fire me and get it over with.*

Rodnicki was nearly bursting. That gum was getting decimated. I wondered how he'd have handled a call from Mr. Dinosaur. How far into that dinner at the Toothaker house would he have put up with?

"Something to the tune of two hundred and fifty thousand dollars over a four-year period."

"Okay," I said. I didn't know if they wanted me to confess or something. "That's a lot of money, Mr. Chessman. Do we know how that happened?"

"We do, Mr. McCall."

He paused. I saw him waiting for Rodnicki, but he was still locked on to a button on my shirt.

Then, he said, "Well, you're the big shit now, good job.

Got what you wanted."

"Andy, this wasn't what we——" Chessman said. He sat up a bit.

"Were you the one that ratted me out?" Rodnicki said. "Jesus, it was just a little off the top. You bloodsuckers. Christ." Rodnicki stood and his office chair rolled back into the bookshelf behind him. Framed pictures fell. A crystal ornament broke on the floor. He was rubbing his head. Chessman also stood and held his planner sturdily at his side.

"Calm down, Andy. We discussed this. We have to inform him, so he can move the unit forward."

If I knew anything, I knew Chessman didn't know Rodnicki. I also knew that Rodnicki wasn't one to be shamed publicly, whether in front of many or one person. And that one person was not going to be me.

"Fucking Lorraine! I told you that. She was the one skimming, okay? Why don't you have her in here? Come on, McCall, tell him that this is all bullshit, yeah?"

I wanted to inject the past two days of my experience into this guy's head. Into Chessman's, too. I started thinking that maybe I shouldn't have burned the videotape Tone-Bone gave me. Should I have found a way to broadcast that? Put it on public access? –No. My mind reeled. I didn't want any of that. The vastness of what the Fuck Offs brought down on us...I couldn't measure, couldn't dispute. But here Andy Rodnicki was getting shit-canned for stealing a quarter of a million. I was likely going next. But I didn't care. Not anymore.

When I paid attention again, Chessman was trying to placate Rodnicki. Something about not prosecuting if the money was paid back within a certain amount of time. He was smiling. It was a cruel smile. One made by those who claim moral victory over those they capture. It was an evil kindergarten teacher's smile.

Rodnicki opened his top drawer where he kept his cigarettes. He spit out his gum onto the desk. Instead of cigarettes, though, he pulled out a .38 and pointed it at Chessman.

"What the fuck are you doing, Andy?" Chessman said.

I felt like I was far away. Watching a movie.

"Lorrain left, with the kids. She knew what was coming. She's gone. She left this on me. But if you're gone, this goes away."

"That's not true, and you know it," Chessman said. "Jesus, Andy, it's just money. Pay it back! If you kill me, you go to prison forever. They'll gas you."

The thought hadn't occurred to Rodnicki. He processed it, considered it acceptable. He held his arm out straighter. The nose of the gun was two feet from Chessman's face. It would've made a hell of a mess on the cinderblock wall behind him. Chessman dropped his planner and papers. He started to plead. Beg. It was like they'd forgotten I was there.

I felt like I could've gotten up and walked out.

I thought: *We're all merely chaos temporarily held back. Our cell walls hold back the juices. Those walls scale up into veins, tissues, organs, skin, skull. We're bags of chaos sauce slopping our meaning into each other's sightlines because our head meat wants more fun drugs. Was pleasure a by-product of pain? Or was pain a by-product of pleasure?*

But all of it gets eaten by Mr. Dinosaur in the end. Today, tomorrow.

I felt like I was in a star god's mouth right then. I almost wanted that thing, that nothing that existed, to clamp down on the whole town. It could've. If it wanted to. But even *it* apparently had an order of operations. The dead first.

(Rodnicki now had a hand behind Chessman's skull and he pushed the gun deeper into the poor guy's mouth. His teeth interfered with the gun's slide inward. Chessman's eyes were pried open with fear. He could barely stand. Rodnicki seemed to be crying and raging simultaneously.)

Everything in the room seemed greasy to me. Everything coated in a fine sheen of slick, oily mucus. It was so alien. But welcome. I'd started to appreciate the gleam of it. I couldn't tell if it was real or not. I didn't care anymore. Yet an undulating tone was in the back of my consciousness. I realized it was my own voice. Looping a phrase. *Stand up. Stand up. Stand up. Stand up. Stand up.*

Stand up.

So I did.

Rodnicki noticed and threatened to kill me next. Chessman whimpered. It smelled bad in the office now. I believed that Chessman had shat himself.

The Loop would come in and out. My will to obey it, oscillating. I could not confirm whether that was because of Mr. Dinosaur or not. I assumed he—it—was behind everything now.

"Where are your kids," I said.

Rodnicki caught off guard. "Huh?"

"The boys."

"They're with Lorraine."

"How would they react if they heard you did this? If you shot Chessman through the head?"

Even the mention of it made Chessman cry out.

Rodnicki was sweating down onto the gun, onto his victim's face. Tears, too.

"Man, you *know* what they'd think!"

"Right, it would not go well for them, Andy. They'd think about this one horrible thing you did for the rest of their lives. And who knows what Lorraine or the public would say. Take the gun out of his mouth. Don't let your kids hear this shit. You fucked up. It can be fixed."

I saw the words melt into his brain and coat it like a gravy. I expected a blast. I expected a spray of meat, blood, bone. The dismemberment of a person's life in front of me.

Instead, Rodnicki pulled the gun like a hook from a fish's mouth.

At that moment, the Loop, the oscillation, tried to get me to say: *Now put it in your mouth.*

Your mouth your mouth your mouth

I had to fight that urge. Hard. My fingernails dug into my palms. I tried to grip the floor through my shoes. I pressed my tongue to the roof of my mouth. I stared at my stolen Mondale/Ferraro '84 button. Chessman's knees connected with the floor: his head hung down. Rodnicki's wrist was tilting upward while his gaze directed out the window and onto some bush or tree.

"Andy. Put the gun on the desk."

I thought he was going to reconsider. Reverse everything and pull the trigger. I felt it.

But he slid the gun over. It was hot. I knew nothing about guns, but I knew how to open it from watching a shitload of *Cagney and Lacy* and *Spencer*. I dumped the bullets into my hand and pocketed them.

"Kurt, stand up and get your shit."

I had to go and pick him up under the armpits, shake him a bit. Understandable. The past few days had given me a resilience to weird fuckery I'd not had before. Where if he'd caught me a week prior, I'd also have emptied my bowels into my slacks.

Rodnicki fell into his roller chair and was crying. I told

him to get it together. Same with Chessman.

"Here's the deal. Rodnicki will pay the money back in installments starting six months from now. Private transactions between him and Starboard." (Every word was fighting its way out of my mouth. The last thing I wanted to do was negotiate on behalf of this rotten asshole who'd made my life a living hell for years.) "Write this down, Chessman. And, here's the important part. *You will not press charges.* Not you, not Starboard."

Kurt Chessman shakily scribbled this into his Franklin Planner. The pen wobbled. He had to flex his hands every so often. Good boy. He affirmed it with me. Rodnicki got it, too, through his thick emotional wall. Good boys, all.

I was waiting for anger to bounce back into Chessman. Retaliation for humiliating him, for nearly killing him, now that the gun was out of play. But that surge of emotion didn't crest. It would surely hit him later in his hotel. When he got it all down, and I made them both sign an unofficial affidavit and gave it to Kurt, I told him to go. Something in his eyes told me *thank you*, but who knows. I tried not to look at him. I felt horrible knowing I had less interest or investment in saving them both than trying *not* to let them die. It was more about trying to restrain that Loop inside me.

"One last thing," I said.

Rodnicki looked up at me. I stepped past him to his corkboard.

I yanked off the Mondale/Ferarro '84 button and pinned it to my shirt. Then I left the office and didn't close the door.

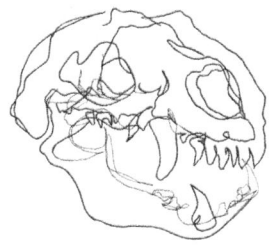

SEVENTEEN

Keller avoided me for the rest of the day at work. That was fine. I expected it. Truth be told, I didn't want to be reminded of the tape or the phone, either. And sitting through Rodnicki's reenactment of *The Deer Hunter* in there wasn't a thrill on top of it all.

At home, that evening, I put a frozen pizza in the oven and lost myself in the TV. I wasn't watching, though. I was thinking.

I thought about how it's a fun thing to do when you're a teenager to pretend like you give zero fucks about life. You may not actually think you're invincible, but there's a sense that life's rules can be bent for you, if needed. All different kinds of faux nihilism are on the menu. I mean, I'd read chunks of Nietzsche in high school, too. But we got it wrong. The so-called miracle of life was located in that sliver of molecular jangling that we were, if we were that at all. In an infinity, we were a slice of stupid. A wriggling flagellating host for mitochondria and DNA.

I repeated that night, eating pizza, an experiment I'd once done many years before. I took what age I thought I'd live to, let's say for argument's sake it would be seventy-eight. I divided it by a few numbers. The first number was the amount of years *Homo sapiens* had been on earth. The second was the number of years scientists estimated the universe had been around. It was basically zero either way. The decimal point followed by all those zeroes was a stark reminder of how little the void acknowledged us. But "acknowledge" wasn't even the right word. More like, in the objective scheme of things, it was as if we'd not even existed at all. I chilled. All over again, I grew cold from this fact. I was, in a sense, already dead. And yet, here was this Mr. Dinosaur coming from above, from outside us, fucking with us. If we humans were so insignificant, then why Earth? Why this state? This city?

Then the goddamn phone rang. Again. This time, I didn't pay attention. I actively ignored it. I did not answer or unplug it. Nothing. Nada. I pretended the phone wasn't there. It would ring, but stop before hitting the machine. It did this every fifteen minutes, for five hours.

After eating most of the pizza (I kept hearing the word *victuals* in my head) and tossing back more than a few beers, I fell asleep in front of the tube. One of the news dudes with helmeted hair was signing off, Koppel or Donaldson. I couldn't tell them apart sometimes.

Finally, the phone quit. And I—was—out.

I had a dream (I think it was a dream) where I could not breathe. That's all it was. My throat closed on me and I stumbled around in this room trying to will my airway to open. I'd had this dream before and was pretty good about noticing it *inside the dream*. So, I could sort of stun myself awake. And it always ended up I was sleeping in a horrible position and was closing off my breathing, encouraging some bad snoring.

But it took me a number of times to stun myself awake, when I realized that—*I was awake*.

I was not in my own room, though. I was standing in someone's bedroom in front of a dresser with all the drawers pulled open. I still couldn't breathe. When I understood where

I was, I gripped my throat. Gasping, I stuck my fingers in my mouth, but I gagged on something. It was cloth. Someone, or me, had shoved a pair of woman's panties and two socks in my mouth. I had to leave, but I didn't know what to do. The room smelled like...perfume. My mouth tasted of it, too. A bottle was opened and empty on the floor. Had I drank it? What the fuck was going on? A digital alarm clock on the dresser announced in red letters that it was 4:47 a.m. It wasn't light outside, but it wasn't totally dark either. I heard a shifting of bed sheets behind me. I turned.

An old man was sat up in the bed, staring at me with his mouth hung down.

"Who are you? What are you doing here? Mikey! Help!"

I scrambled, but didn't know where to go. I heard clomping footsteps from either downstairs or upstairs. I had no idea even which floor I was on. I tried to apologize and also back out, but I didn't want to run into "Mikey," whoever that may be. They didn't sound gentle. As I felt my way through the dark hallway, I saw odds and ends of pictures, torn and ripped. Like bite marks from a dog. But I knew that it had been me. My stomach suddenly felt weighted, full. I wanted to puke. A dumped over ashtray. A wooden crucifix gnawed on. A whole pile of half-eaten and destroyed shit in the middle of the living room. I felt like I was insane.

"What-the-fuck?" I heard from behind me. There was

a guy on the stairs. Massive. His shadow loomed, and I froze.

"I'm not a robber. I don't know how I got here."

I was going to hurl.

"McCall?"

The urge to vomit took a back seat to spinal fear. The hall light flipped on and there on the staircase was Big Tiny Keller. In Chicago Bears pajamas.

"Mikey, should I call the police?" the old man said from the bedroom.

"Yeah, dad. I mean, no. Don't call. It's okay. I think..."

Keller's father padded out shielding his eyes from the light. When he saw the mangled pile of possessions, a wail slipped from his mouth. "*Margaret.*"

Big Tiny pointed to the pile.

"McCall, what the fuck are you doing in my house? What is this?"

"Tiny, I have no idea how I got here. Honestly, I was in my apartment, eating dinner, I went to bed. Maybe I'd had a few too many beers, but I don't sleepwalk. I mean—I don't—I'm sorry, Keller."

"Michael, do you know this idiot?" his father said.

"I do. He's my boss."

"What's in god's creation is he doing here? Did you let him in?"

"No."

This confused the father. I was sure that if his boss,

who I'm certain was a roughneck, had ever toddled into his home like a somnambulistic psychopath in the middle of the night, he'd have a metric shit-ton of questions and demands. His father wiped his nose. I looked into his eyes. I knew what I had done. I could feel the queerness of carpet, chemicals, and wood settling in my guts. I wondered how I would shit it out. Would I die? Did I need my stomach pumped? I wanted to say that a certain thing from beyond the realm of human understanding called Mr. Dinosaur made me do it. It made me eat your wife's possessions. And though that would've been the truth, I know he'd have me locked up as fast as he could dial the county Sheriff's office.

Keller stood by his father. He wore a silver hoop in the left ear. He must have taken it out when he worked. And I could see skull and titty tattoos up and down his arms which were usually masked by chef's whites. He looked like a linebacker-in-training with that Bears get-up.

Then he open-hand slapped me in the face.

I fell hard. Like a dropped bag of cans.

Boom.

Done.

The world rang: a dull shitty gong. I saw double for a sec. Then I recovered, sort of. Both men helped me up. The father asked if he should call the cops. Keller said no. He told him to get some bourbon instead. "But nothing good. The cheap stuff. McCall doesn't deserve it." We drank it in silence in the dining room, all three looking at the pile I'd unconsciously amassed. I began to cry and feel sick. I wanted to vomit right there. The father cried, too, but not for me. Keller said her death had been sudden and raw for his father. And here I'd violated that long grief with such deplorable inhumanity. Keller escorted me outside for "fresh air."

"I'm sorry. I didn't know you lived with your dad."

"You would've done this anyway?"

"No, I—"

"I thought when we burned that tape and the phone, Cade, that this shit was done with."

"I did, too. Listen, Tiny, I can't say why I'm here. What I'm doing. Yesterday Rodnicki pulled a gun on the investigator and almost killed the guy. If it wasn't for me, that office would be a murder scene."

Keller couldn't believe me. I knew that. I explained the scene, the outcome. Told him to keep it to himself for now. Likely I'd get Rodnicki's spot and work would be, maybe, smoother.

Keller gestured up and down at me, like, *what about your weird ass habit of showing up in places you don't belong?*

"I found you with your head in the trash compactor, Cade. That's not normal. Now you're in my house, eating my dead mother's possessions. What-in-the-fuck? Are you going to say it's this shit with Mr. Dinosaur? You are, aren't you? I can see it in your eyes."

I nodded. I knew it was. He knew it was. He was rationalizing, though.

We were putting off what we knew we were going to do. We turned to the burn barrel at the rear, by the fence. It was now light enough to see, and the sun would be up in a few minutes. Smoke curled up from the barrel. Barely. Probably embers buried under ash. There was a metal poker leaning against the cyclone. Slowly we walked to the barrel. Keller grabbed the poker.

The phone and tape were gone. Not a slag or remnant of melted plastic. Nothing.

"Good work, McCall. I have no idea what you've done, but this is heinous."

"What do we do?"

He stabbed the poker into the yard's dirt. Shoved it as deep as possible.

"Tone-Bone. She's the only one who knows what this is. But I'm not calling her. She won't answer, and if she did, she'd tell us to take a hike. Get your shit and let's go."

I looked around. "I have no shit."

"Then let's ramble."

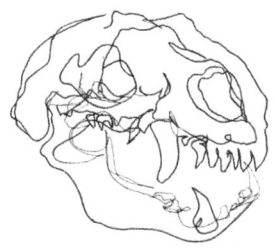

EIGHTEEN

We sped through the dawn back down those depleted, empty, rural roads and cut-thrus and abandoned frontage roads and obscured access paths. This time Mellencamp sounded lonely, scared. Living in a small town was not a sign of pride. It was a curse.

Last time, I didn't know where we were in the dark. Daylight didn't help my sense of direction. After thirty minutes, Keller made a turn too quickly. His muscle memory must've quit him. There were no trees. Only a massive clearing in the woods. He slowed. Coming down what I learned was the last road to Tone-Bone's house, Keller stopped.

"Are we lost, or...?"

He pointed past me out the window.

I'd seen this before. Crop circles on TV. Except those things were done in grass, wheat, corn. This was...*everything*. That's why I didn't remotely recognize the road or landscape.

Where Tone-Bone's house should've been was devastation.

Everything had been flattened as if by a geometrically precise tornado. An orderly swirl. Smashed. Trees at the base, snapped. Grasses and plants, crushed and smoothed like a boy's slicked hair. At the same time, I had a vision of a massive creature cropping the surface of the earth with its maw, a massive bone machine eating the face of humanity right off like a flimsy scab. Mr. Dinosaur was an above-ground bone machine with no off switch or emergency brake. Tone-Bone's house could've as easily been smashed by a massive dinosaur tail, really. Jesus.

Keller jumped out and ran to where her cabin's steps once were. He started thrashing at and threshing the rubble underneath the vegetation. Tone-Bone's entire life crunched under my shoe soles. The air smelled like mown hay, sweet and damp.

I scanned the tree lines surrounding us. I kept seeing movement. Leaves rustling. Saplings wobbling. I heard rushy sounds in the bushes and undergrowth. Like something large moving beyond. We heard a distant sound. The high grinding whine of a buzz saw. But then it could've been an angry cow lowing. Or an air horn. All the sounds mixed together.

The sun should've broken fully over the horizon by this point. I felt suspended in some kind of early morning sleeplessness.

"What does this?" I asked.

Keller threw clobbered kitchen items or smashed furniture parts into the air. Even the smallest bits of her house were broken into tinier pieces. Like whatever did this wasn't happy with demolishing the surrounds. It was unmappable. Weather couldn't perpetrate this. Nor could animals. Maybe not even humans at their most driven. I worried for her dogs, the innocents. Poor doggos. Who knows? Maybe they fled or were mucking around in the woods prior to the Flattening.

"Here."

Keller rose and stepped back from a blackened spot.

It was the tape and phone we'd taken and burned in the barrel.

"I did not do that sweet jeezus."

"Neither did I."

"That's impossible."

"Well."

I didn't say it then, but I thought: *Maybe they aren't the same ones. Not the same tape and phone.* But they were, they were. Keller descended upon the phone and broke open the housing. He curled his fingers around the bell and yanked it out. No noise. But I knew that if I picked up the cream-colored receiver, that crackling, staticky, distant voice of Mr. Dinosaur would be there to greet me.

"Keep the bell," I said. "This time I'm taking both."

I bundled both under my arms.

A tree fell in the distance. The slow, sharp initial crack, then the forever-lasting sound of a whole tree breaking cell by cell, snapping and creaking its way down into the forest floor with a slow *whoof*. This was two hundred yards away. Birds didn't flutter. Animals didn't make a sound.

We were in the middle of a flat circle that started to feel more like a bullseye than a message.

"I'm sorry about your friend."

Keller pretended not to hear me.

"Let's skedaddle," he said.

We didn't say another word the whole way back. And still the sun took forever to rise.

We decided to eat breakfast at a small trucker highway stop right outside of town. They must've had a pancake genius back there on the flattop grill. When Big Tiny Keller dropped me off at my place, I thanked him. He nodded. If I was ever in his home again, he said, he would severely maim me. Understood. He said he might skip work today. I said: Do it.

"I understand if you don't want to start a business with me anymore," I said. I was joking, sort of. Who wanted to work after this nonsense?

"You better start a catering business, McCall. I don't want to stay at Starboard forever. Christ. What do I look like, a glutton for punishment?"

Mellencamp sang "R.O.C.K. in the U.S.A." as he drove off.

I didn't sweat not getting into work on time that morning. After what I did for Rodnicki? I could come in when I wanted to. Same for Keller.

Standing outside my apartment door, I heard my phone ringing. Behind me, a neighbor taking out the trash said, in a shitty tone, that it had been ringing all night. I dropped Tone-Bone's videotape and the haunted phone into my sink and placed a hand on my own incessant phone.

I answered it, expecting the devil.

Instead, one of my best chefs. He sounded frantic. "Jesus, Cade. We've been calling you for the last hour, where you been?"

"What the hell's going on?"

"Rodnicki shot himself. Blew his head off in the walk-in freezer. Nancy found him while she was opening. She 'bout had a heart attack." Caught embezzling, and with his family leaving him, Rodnicki killed himself. It was and wasn't a surprise. My legs failed, and I slid along my cabinets to the floor. "There're detectives here now. Took them forever to get here. Said there was a bunch of break-ins all over town, and with the second explosion at Golden Forest...well, anyway, they want you to come down."

"Of course," I said. I hung up.

A dark thought, but all I could worry about was how much inventory would be wasted because Rodnicki exploded his blood splatter, brains, and skull matter on it. Even in death, he was a selfish prick.

Something else nagged me. The neighbor lady said that my phone had been ringing off the hook "all night." Not only the past hour. The phone was ringing when I passed out the night before. And who knows what it did while I "sleepwalked" to Keller's. I ignored it, thinking it was Mr. Dinosaur, but—*what if it wasn't?*

The answering machine light blipped. Still greasy. I pressed it. The first message was crying and heavy breathing. A second the same. A third with muffled wailing.

Rodnicki.

Had to have been after I was out. A fourth was whimpering and quiet pleading for it to stop. I couldn't tell if Andy was talking to me or someone in the room with him. These escalated in tone and anxiety. I forced myself to listen to them all. I was convinced he was talking to someone else. And I knew that, on some level, Mr. Dinosaur was going to want to eat Andy Rodnicki. All I could hope is that that thing didn't want me to serve my boss up in a chafing dish.

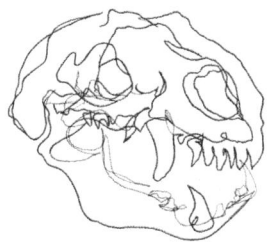

NINETEEN

Before I confronted the horror at work, I went to the sink. I set the disconnected and indestructible phone on the counter. The tape next to it. They were like beacons. I wanted to destroy them. Rid myself of them forever, but I could not. Like old family photos you know you'll rarely, if ever, look at, I could not bear to hurt them.

And then I wondered something human. Something fragile and naïve.

I wondered if I could negotiate or persuade what wasn't of this world.

Could I persuade Mr. Dinosaur to go away? I'd persuaded Rodnicki not to kill Chessman. That worked. I couldn't do anything to stop him turning the gun on himself, though.

I picked up the receiver and the cold plastic kissed my ear. There was, as I said there would be, a humming and crackling on the "line." I told whoever was listening that I wanted them to leave me alone and those around me. There was no response.

Not at first. But then what felt like air or wind leaked from the sound holes in the phone receiver. The phone was actually cold now; I hadn't imagined it. Frost steamed from the top and bottom. A whispering was deep in the phone, deep on the line.

The voice was Tone-Bone's. She was testing the line. Hello? Hello?

"Tone-Bone? Is that you? It's Cade McCall."

Hurt to have the phone so close to my skin.

"They want you to cater an event, Cade. Need you to come."

"Who?"

"The Fuck Offs, Cade. They came to get me. To save me. To save you."

She told me to meet her and the remnants of the biker gang that night at the Toothaker Estate. She said that we could quiet Mr. Dinosaur.

It was a long day. The detectives had no question that it was suicide. One weird thing happened when they asked me to review the security footage with them, though. (Well, not weird. It was expected. Expected the same way I knew someone was standing between the vending machines at the library.)

We were huddled over a small television screen in the manager's office. The camera pointed right at the bank of walk-in freezers. One door was open. Rodnicki slumped against the wall, gun in mouth. I did not want to watch, but the detectives sort of pressured me into it with their bored stares. Rodnicki was screaming like a cow on its way to the slaughterhouse. He pulled the trigger. The back of his head slowly spread out behind him on the stainless steel. A liquid nest. Vaporized consciousness. I wanted to vomit. I chewed it back.

I asked why the footage was in slow motion. It seemed cruel.

A detective turned to me. Surprised, yet bored. "It's not."

That meant the bullet moved through his head slug-slow when Andy thought it would all end like a flash and instead he spider-webbed his head over two minutes. Slow-motion suicide. I wasn't sure about all this but didn't want to stir it up with the police and had no way to say that sometimes a person can be pushed to kill themselves and it's not really "taking your own life," but rather "giving in to the atmospheric pressures that are only obeying the distant pulses and waves that emanate from so far away in the universe that there's no imagination mutant enough to hug it alive."

Yeah. So. Hard decisions.

I decided to trash all the food from the walk-in freezer and cleaned it myself.

Tina Ramsey, the one and only, arrived near the end of this. Headphones on. Guitars banging away. Sharp synth hits. I pointed at my ears.

"Cocteau Twins," she said. The last of the blood was thinned by mop water. She knelt by me. "Need help?"

I handed her a sponge. We worked in silence while Elizabeth Fraser whooped and crooned in the headphones. When we finished, Tina took my hand and we walked outside. We sat on the loading dock, legs hanging over the edge. She lit a clove cigarette. We shared it. I held her hand. She squeezed it.

We didn't say much beyond small grunts of acknowledgment as we smoked or nodded at the music. But after she stubbed out the smoke, she said, "I told you to leave that place."

"I know."

"You needed the money, though?"

I nodded. She pursed her lips in resigned understanding. The music ended. She pushed her Walkman and headphones to me. As a parting gesture? A thank you? An apology? Then she leaned in and we kissed. It was, for me, as I hoped it was for her, the culmination of years of looks, hugs, laughs. Time spent driving around listening to music and trying to live in the space between songs. But I knew she was the last lacerating opportunity to partake in humanity for a long time, if ever. She felt like she knew that, too. So I made it count.

She tasted like clove, orange peel, ash.

My own mouth tasted of nothing.

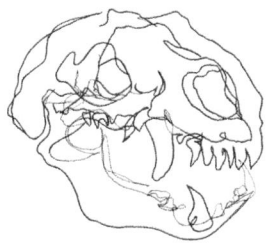

TWENTY

Since there was no menu, I brought nothing to the Toothaker but myself. The Fuck Offs didn't really want a catering gig the way you or I would think of it. This was different. All day I'd heard and felt this pulsating in the air. Like a small drum being struck in the distance. A resonating thump. It had been with me since the day I answered that goddamn message on the machine. I only noticed it now. It had been with me all along. It still persisted when I came in the back door of the estate.

Six Fuck Offs stood around the kitchen island. Some

shaved heads. Long braids. Sharpened teeth, tats, lots of metal pierced in non-standard places. Tight leather jackets with their name in Gothic script on the back. They looked drained, re-animated from epic death. For all I knew, they likely were. Two smoked. Three drank whisky from bottles. They seemed allergic to life. Angry that cigarettes weren't motorcycles. Tone-Bone, the seventh member, lounged in the doorway. We then all sat at the long table where I'd served Mr. Dinosaur.

They explained that they'd been elsewhere. Though they wouldn't say where. Their eyes, what passed as eyes, seemed to say that it was nowhere I wanted to visit any time soon. Tone-Bone said that they required me to serve parts of various items in future catering gigs as payment for Mr. Dinosaur's dormancy. This was its one request. (I wondered if that meant that I could negotiate or persuade it.) I was to commence a slow and steady seeding, a sowing of what, to me, were cultic or occult items. One of the bikers brought in a leather and studded pannier from her bike. She opened the flap in a ceremonial way and began laying out a series of nine objects. I felt thinner in their presence. That is, less three-dimensional. I would never know what it was like to be a 2-D thing, a flat paper cutout, but sitting among those objects for the first time, it was as close as I'd get.

I feel I don't have to say this, but they were all strange and unearthly things. One was a slime that stood and strained and then fell. I don't know, even now, what it responds to or if it's sentient. There were odd pieces of small, heavy metals that disappeared when I turned them sideways, even though I still should've been able to see them from that angle. The hardest to fathom was a ball of absolute darkness, like a piece of the visual field had been cut out. It had no borders, no surface. No way to hold it. Then—two jars. In one: the bright smoke. In the other: cold fire. I cried then. But quietly, so as not to shake their brittle and evil demeanor.

One of the women walked up to me. She seemed... kind? Her fangs pressed into her bottom lip. She reached a finger out and swiped my tears. They hung fat on the tip. She licked them.

They handed me a special knife to cut these objects with. I wasn't to worry about running out of the objects. They would last. I tried humor. "I bet the knife doesn't need sharpening," I said. No one broke a smile. Tone-Bone said I was to secret them into all the food I served until, well, just until. Casseroles and cakes, soups and chowders, muffins and scrambled eggs. Children's birthday cakes, retirees' steaks, wedding appetizers.

The young, the old, the infirm, the boisterous, the quiet.

After they roared away on their motorcycles, I leaned my head onto the table and wept.

Every tear that fell from me landed on the table and, in

time, like mercury slid toward the nine objects where my salt water was absorbed by them.

They were near impossible to carry to the car and home.

Big Tiny Keller worked with me a little longer but he had to quit when his father died. I think he gave up being a chef to ink people. Tina found her way into graduate school in California. She wrote a letter joking about me going out there with her. And I wanted to. But. I didn't want to drag her into my hell. It was the only time we communicated after the loading dock. I wore her headphones all the time from then on. It kept—keeps—the world delineated.

Even when the world breaks in, like when Billy Ballantyne called and demanded we have breakfast at Smitty's. To, you know, catch up. Get friendly. When he got up halfway through his pancakes to take a piss, I had to. I had to slice a piece of the absolute darkness and metal shape. I had to push them into his food. I also had to look away from him for the rest of the meal. I couldn't watch him swallow it down. He thought I was being an asshole, I'm sure. Better that way.

I move often. I have to.

I can't stand the guilt. Of seeing those I feed driving around with Mr. Dinosaur's objects seeding inside of them. I know one day they'll churn, reel, revel, burn, suck, explode.

I don't know exactly when, but they will wake up, yawn, and rise. Those seeds.

And when they do, I hope you're far away from me.

Far, far away from anything remotely human.

ACKNOWLEDGMENTS

The idea for this story arrived on a walk last fall. The image of a shrouded man eating strange objects appeared in my mind, and I went to write it in my Notes app on my phone. As I did, a small spider crawled up over the top of my screen and down onto my finger. I have no idea where it came from. I set it into the grass. I could only see it as a sign to move forward with this particular story. (And I don't put stock into signs and wonders.) So, I'd like to thank that spider. And I'd like to thank Scott Cole for his patience and guidance in the vast world of book design. Erin Al-Mehairi for her care and attention to the prose. Ryan Dunn for his crazy eye for collage. And Claudia Lundahl for her drawing—which she does with eyes closed the first time around! Finally, thanks to my two boys for their ideas and love, and my wife, Katie, who is always willing to watch horror movies with me.

ABOUT THE AUTHOR

Kyle Winkler lives in northeastern Ohio. His writing has appeared in *Conjunctions*, *The Rupture*, *The Millions*, *The Rumpus*, and elsewhere. He teaches writing for Kent State University - Tuscarawas.

kylewinkler.net
@bleakhousing